# ALIEN MANUSCRIPTS, ONYX CUBES & RUNES

Of Ancient Markers & Engineered Genes

Darryl Gopaul

## ALIEN MANUSCRIPTS, ONYX CUBES & RUNES OF ANCIENT MARKERS & ENGINEERED GENES

*iUniverse books may be ordered through booksellers or by contacting:*

*iUniverse*
*1663 Liberty Drive*
*Bloomington, IN 47403*
*www.iuniverse.com*
*1-800-Authors (1-800-288-4677)*

*ISBN: 978-1-5320-8557-4 (sc)*
*ISBN: 978-1-5320-8558-1 (e)*

*Library of Congress Control Number: 2019916164*

*Print information available on the last page.*

*iUniverse rev. date: 10/17/2019*

Archaeological markers and the role of genetics from an anthropological perspective are the basis for this story.

*This book is dedicated to followers of science fiction (especially my immediate family who enjoy this genre). To Daphne Alice, my wife, who has assisted with editing this manuscript.*

# A SPECIAL RECOGNITION

To Derek Johnson, a friend and colleague for over four decades. He has used his company resources to support this author by marketing my books to his customers. I am totally indebted to him.

# CONTENTS

## Section IV

## Section V

# SECTION I

# INTRODUCTION

"Computer, Open Paragraph and Take down This Dictation"

In a cluttered office of a small suburban home in a city outside a major industrial capital, an elderly couple who have lived together for many years sat in old comfortable chairs. With cups of hot tea in their hands, they discussed profound topics of relative unimportance. They were retired.

In their one-storey home set amidst park-like garden surroundings, they were in the habit of receiving small boxes and packages from a friend who owned a commercial business. Invariably these contained gifts of science fiction books and scientific catalogs, usually accompanied with a gift card to the nearby coffee and doughnut store. It was a legacy dated back some fifteen years earlier when the owner of the scientific company asked his scientist friend to assist him by visiting the research institutes in his university town.

These old friends had known each other for decades and had a great time whenever they met because they had a past culture to share. This was a good part-time consulting position job for the retired professor, whose income was adequate for his and his wife's retirement but who needed to reduce the principal of their outstanding line of credit. The couple had decided many years earlier to let their two children have their legacy in advance and began using a small part of the equity in their home towards that end.

Today the doorbell rang, and the wife got up to see who was at the front door. She found a cardboard box on the front step, delivered by a well-known courier. She placed the box on the desk in their office. Her husband had dressed after his shower. They both set about to opening the box with smiles on their faces. They loved receiving gifts from their friend, and like geriatric kids, they wanted to know what surprise was waiting for them.

It was their second coffee break as they carefully cut the tape off the box. It was the wife who paused and said, "This is not from Derek, you know!"

"Why do you say that? What do you mean?" her husband asked. He stopped cutting the tape that held the box shut.

"Well, look," she replied, "his company sticker is not there!" They both took a second look at the outside of the box. There were no indicators or labels that would suggest who the sender might be.

"Oh heck! It is addressed to me. Let us open it anyway," the old man replied.

They opened the box. Within it they found a large old manuscript bound in a leather and copper-like material with a small keyhole, in which was a tiny key. They placed it on the desk. The wife, who had her arm stuck deep in the box, withdrew a wrapped parcel that had several black onyx cubes inside. There were tiny, thread-like white markings like runes on the surface of each cube, undecipherable at first glance.

# CHAPTER 1

# Ancient Manuscripts, Donor Unknown

"Once upon a time, the cosmos was explored by aliens unknown to earthlings, the dominant primate species on a planet called Earth. Earth belonged to a small solar system that had several other planets with no discernable living biological life forms. This small solar system was located at the edge of the Milky Way," wrote the old professor-now-author.

He continued, "Documents uncovered by archaeologists buried in the sands of ancient Egypt, as well as under the South American pyramids, reveal precise structures that primitive earthlings had neither the knowledge nor the technology to erect. It is safe to surmise that these were built by an advanced civilization which modern earthlings refer to as 'extraterrestrial beings.' It is also possible that an advanced early society of humankind had lived, prospered then perished. No one knows, and no supporting evidence has been uncovered at the time of the writing this novel."

His mind cogitated. This is the situation: an unknown author who has published over twenty manuscripts, scientific papers and books of fiction and non-fiction received a box and a brown envelope delivered to his door. He opened it in his office. He had a wry smile on his face, always wishing that there would be a financial offer in the form of a check having come from a well-known movie director asking for the rights to his books, in particular his sci-fi trilogy that had taken him well over twelve years to complete.

With the author having no overt means of marketing or promoting his books, the charlatans who take advantage of first-time authors had called him many times for the promised privilege of selling the books. The catch, as always, was that he had to provide a financial advance to kick off their sales pitch. These parasites thrived on the labour of hard-working authors, and their numbers appeared to have increased over the past twenty years. However, what they do is acceptable to the law, which leaves old writers and poor ones vulnerable.

After emptying the contents on his desk, the old man found fragile documents had come from an unknown source. A scribbled note suggested the need for review and interpretation, but his critical mind thought right away that this was a hoax promulgated by someone who knew him well. He was about to discard the contents into the nearby shredder basket under his desk but paused. He and his wife had left these contents unopened near the junk mail bin. Looking through his window at his neighbours' rooftops, his mind drifted as curiosity, along with the imagination typical of a storyteller, entered his mind. He pulled out the remaining two packages from the box and found a heavy manila envelope and a box one foot square and four inches deep. He laid these items on his desk.

His wife said that she was off shopping, but if she had remained any longer she would have tossed the lot out as she did with junk mail and deleted unwanted telephone calls with offers. At their age, they had become tired of junk mail cluttering up the recycle bins every week.

The author saw the red SR5 SUV pull into the driveway about an hour later. He would be needed to bring in the bags of groceries that his better half had bought. He left the two unopened packages on his desk and headed towards the front door to help his wife with the laden bags.

She had her walking stick with her. He questioned, "Why do we have to buy so much food? It is only two of us living here. We no longer do any entertaining, and we no longer have any ambulatory friends or family." Almost all the friends with whom they socialized after retirement used to meet at a local Greek restaurant for breakfast. Most of those people were no longer around, and those who were not dead were too lame to emerge from their homes. In the end, a few said they no longer enjoyed eating out because their teeth were not that good—and anyway they had lost their sense of taste. Over time their friends, who once had given support to each other disappeared. This old professor who was a lab scientist had taken up writing science fiction stories, which gave him great personal satisfaction, using his time on the demanding profession of novelist. However, while his books looked good to him after they were printed, he spent no time marketing them.

He left his books, which could be found in the marketplace of the large high-tech emporiums, but there was no sales engine behind marketing his work. He often fantasized that a movie producer would call him and give an advance of money for the rights to his book and produce a movie. He also daydreamed that he would get a small royalty income that would allow him to continue to publish his books under his own logo.

Such are the dreams of those who write, but their passion outweighs any and all financial necessity. This particular gentleman wrote because he loved to write, and his creative dreams found a niche in the world where they would survive for aeons. "The written word will never disappear from our libraries. These words will wait silently for their time to come and serve the use for which they were created" was one of his oft-made comments. His wife of 53 years encouraged his pastime because she derived passive enjoyment as her keen mate never hesitated to tell her the direction or plot of his work.

She invariably looked into his eyes smiled but never commented either positively or negatively. He never knew whether she was interested or just offered enough attention for him to continue. But quietly, she let his words melt into nothingness giving no response.

However, every author knows intuitively, that they will always be alone. It was rare to have a companion that would actively and enthusiastically encourage their writing. The female spouse of a well-known author when asked what her role was in his creative writing after his demise. She quietly said, "How does one contribute to a creative art in one who has inherited it mysteriously?"

## A Gift of Old Manuscripts

With his wife handing him a cup of tea, the old man sat down as she opened the manila envelope first to reveal a brown age beaten leather binder that contained yellowed papyrus sheets with black line drawings. She cautiously handled the heavy book with small metal hinges that kept the hundred pages in order. These pages were not numbered. She laid them out on his desk. With a pair of scissors, she carefully scored the sealant sticky seals of the envelope. The lids of the box folded over and within were several stone squares that were blackened as though scorched by fire.

They both laid out the dozen blocks on the surface of the old wooden desk noting the scribbling of non-English language. The wife thought at first that it might be Sanskrit.

They both tried to search out the post mark and the writing on the box directed to his name only. They searched for any kind of information that would indicate from whom these artifacts came or some description as to where they might have originated. Their search was fruitless, so the husband said, "Ah, leave it on the desk. I shall make a call to the university in the morning to try to find out who might be able to assist us. Hopefully someone can explain what these artifacts are and suggest who there was around who would follow up on their value, if any, in the archaeology department."

The wife carefully replaced the square cubic rocks back into the box and closed the lid. She resealed the manila envelope with the binder. They sat down and quietly sipped their tea.

This couple were entering their eighth decade and were accustomed to the little rituals of mid-afternoon tea with a shared butter scone on one half and the other having either strawberry jam or honey from their friend's farm. She usually told her husband what she had bought for supper that evening. Today she quietly said, "You know, Dear, I was able to get a cow's tongue at the grocery."

He stopped sipping his tea and looked up at his grey-haired wife sitting opposite him. "You did? How come the grocery had a fresh tongue? It is fresh, isn't it?"

"Yes! Yes! I was casually looking at the meat counter when I saw the tongue, so I asked the butcher girl behind the counter if it was for sale. She said a customer had ordered one but two were shipped. I have only just unpacked it about an hour ago. Are you interested?"

Without waiting for his reply, she added, "I told her to wrap it up for me. It is a really large one, so I will begin boiling it now. I also bought a fresh Italian white rye loaf."

With that his wife got up and took the teacups away, saying, "I shall begin right away. I also bought a new bottle of cloves to stick over the tongue."

"Ho! Splendid. I know what we shall have for supper instead of a roast: large sandwiches loaded with cold tongue a little mustard. Yes, I shall open that bottle of Shiraz that Martin bought for my birthday."

It was 1:30 in the afternoon. The old author got up and decided to take a chance and call the local university. He had a colleague still employed well past his retirement age who was in charge of the ancient literature library. They had met when he and his wife had donated their original copies of Goldsmith leather-bound books to the university library. They decided that they should slowly begin to downsize their belongings in the house in which they had lived for fifty plus years. Much to their surprise the Library was pleased to receive these first texts by this ancient author that would complete their collection.

They continued to downsize their home furnishing: Much of the teak furniture was given away to their daughters while others were sent off to Goodwill Industries. Their library comprised many dated university text books from six decades ago as well as loads of paperbacks and the works of old and at one time contemporary authors. Included in their library were books from their global travels.

Many of the paperbacks were donated to the local church bazaars, they also gave away the remaining copies of his own published books. The old couple had discussed should one of them die first, it would be too much work for the other to empty the house before putting it up for sale. When it came to the books they had offered their library of books to their daughters and quite a few were taken away. But printed books had become de rigueur, as youths of two generations passed were reading from electrical portable devices.

Books in the early part of this the twenty first century were slowly becoming an anachronism. Thank goodness for the University Archivist, who had come to their home to review their donations before he took away the antique books. They were provided with an official certificate as donors to the libraries at the University. That gentleman had remained a colleague that they could call on in when needed. The old man took up the telephone and called the archivist and was passed through almost immediately.

"Yes, Robert," Les spoke to his contact. "It is a bit unusual to have these old manuscripts and artifacts in my possession." He smiled, looking through the office window. "None whatsoever. We looked, and there were no identification marks. One wondered if this was some sort of prank. We have no idea from whom or from where or what period or even if they are genuine." The telephone conference paused, followed by silence.

He picked up his diary and turned to the date. "You can come over this evening? That is wonderful. We shall be looking forward to your scholarly advice and sincere conversation since we do not get enough of that. Yes, see here, we shall have tea and bit of a surprise for you to snack on. See you then."

The old writer sat down and carefully wrote down in his day diary the appointment with the archivist Robert from the university library for 5:30 p.m

# CHAPTER 2

# Research Leads to Knowledge

"As usual, my dear, that was a splendid cup of tea. Orange pekoe?" Robert the archivist chatted with his two old friends, donors of rare books to his department. There was a smile on his mustachioed face.

The warm-hearted Alice smiled. "Oh! You do know your tea!" She continued, "In fact it is a non-decaffeinated brand with pekoe and a blend of Earl Grey. We find it quite pleasing. What do you think of my sandwiches?"

Robert responded immediately, "Well, old chaps, on entering the sunroom I smelt the aroma of cloves and a hint of beef flavorings. My heart fluttered as I thought, *Not that old English standby. No, she could never get that locally!* As soon as I tasted it, my eyes closed. Warm ox tongue sandwiches with a mild English mustard on that crusty rye—absolute heaven. May I have another, please?"

Les responded quickly, "Of course you can, Robert. And you are quite correct about getting this tongue. One usually has to order it directly from the butcher one week in advance, but not today. My lovely wife was just in time at the butcher's and was surprised to see one in the fridge. On enquiry, she was told the fresh tongue was left by a customer who had ordered one, but two were shipped. She took it immediately." There was a brief silence as the three contented elderly folks sipped at their cups of tea.

Robert opened his eyes and said, "Ah! Les, you have the goods. Let us have a look." The two old men were seated cups of tea in front of them, as Robert quietly looked around the inside of the envelope and in the box. He carefully, almost tenderly, withdrew the manuscript from the leather-bound metal album. He scanned the pages, looking at and feeling their texture. He then opened the album near the back. Again he felt the texture of the page while bending his ear close to the rubbing sound of his fingers.

Taking the box of square stones to the end of the sunroom, which had more light, Robert opened the box after searching around the sides, bottom and top. Slowly he removed each blackened square in scripted onyx stone, examining each carefully. Then, to the old couple's surprise, he withdrew a jeweller's loupe from his coat pocket, fitted it to his eye and searched around the little scratches and markings. The room remained quiet, the patience of the old to remain still, until these oddities were fully surveyed and microscopically scrutinized by the master detective. This was essential.

Robert carefully placed the stones back into the box and, looking at his hosts and leaving the items on the table, remained silent. The couple felt that the items were being scrutinized by an expert literary archaeologist. Robert remained quiet, sitting and looking at his briefcase on the floor near his chair. He reached down, pulled out a small tablet and switched it on. He absent-mindedly reached for his cup of tea, looking up at Les and Alice. After a prolonged silence, he said, "Les, this was addressed to you?"

"Yes, Robert, but I have no idea who would send such pieces of antiquity to me," Les replied.

"Do you think these are genuine artifacts?" Les asked.

Robert responded, "I have no idea from where these items originated or from which archaeological site or museum they've come from, or which period of time from which they might have been recovered. They could have been raided from several sites on the planet. The wars in the Middle East have decimated many of the ancient sites that were under different stages of study by universities from around the free world. I may have a few ideas, but I must do a quick search into the archives of the Greek and Persian museums just to screen out a few mental conflicts as to location. These are genuine ancient artifacts, not a ruse to annoy you."

Robert quietly stared up his tablet and again went into a concentrated silence. This was a cue for Les and Alice to quietly remove the empty teapot and the small decorative plates and take them into the kitchen. Les looked across the room at the old papyrus drawing of an Egyptian queen. It had hung there for well over fifty years. He and his wife had collected it when they travelled through the turmoil of the Middle East at the end of the last century. They had visited as scientific ambassadors with a group of intellectuals from several universities in Canada, the USA and other South American countries.

Les was the chosen leader of the group, whose mission was to visit universities, their faculties and public health facilities in Egypt—the cities of Cairo and Alexandria—then go onto Israel's main cities, Tel Aviv, Jerusalem and Bethlehem. Included in these visits were the Wailing Wall, Bethlehem and the holy sites of the Church of the Nazarene, the Dome of the Rock and the White Mosque, followed by a fleeting trip to Constantinople in Turkey. All were on the academic agenda.

Strange, after all this time, Les still could not understand why he, a Canadian and British professional, had been asked to be the leader. He had been asked by the American Ambassador Program, as it was then, to lead a small group of 16 participants. As usual when they travelled, he collected a number of small items, some touristy in nature, such as carvings of the stable at the birth of baby Jesus, from olive wood. This particular item depicted the scene of the kings, shepherds and animals in the manger. It sits permanently in their sitting room, where it has been for 50 years.

Robert's hoarse voice broke into Les's reverie: "Les, this is an unknown artifact on this planet. I have contacted the experts around the countries where there might be a relationship, as well as the British Museum of Antiquities. They were all stunned at what you have. And strange as it may seem, none of them asked for the items to be sent to them. Indeed, after seeing my cellphone photos of the items, they all said that I should delete the pictures as soon as possible; only the person to whom the parcel was addressed should have these artifacts. No reason was given, and no one offered their services, which is equally strange to me."

Les was joined by his aproned wife, who'd heard everything Robert had said. "They were addressed to you," Robert said to Les. "And while it sounds strange that they are not items natural to Earth's environment, these experts stressed 'on this planet.' It seems that these items are yours to keep to study and do with as you choose."

Robert continued, "I did not ask for your permission, and having the responses from agencies that I have dealt with for many years, I am disappointed. I sent an enquiry for information on unusual artifacts to all the reputable agencies on earth."

Robert turned around to look at the vacant screen of his tablet, as if hoping something would appear. He continued, "Their official responses will come to me over the next day or so, and I will pass them onto you. I am sorry I could not have been of more assistance. Should more information come to me, I shall get in touch with you immediately. Thanks for including me on this most mysterious group of items. I must head home before the traffic builds up. There is a show at the Avon Theatre. My wife has cautioned that I be at home in time for us to attend."

As he stood up to put his coat on, he explained, "The traffic from here to my little town can be quite horrific, but it is still early enough. If I leave now, I should beat the rush home." Turning to Alice, he said, "Thanks for the lovely tea, my dear." Speaking to them both, he continued, "You two are really great chaps to know. Sitting and chatting with you both brings back memories of my English grandparents who guided my parents' lives and my own for many years.

"You both remind me of the scholarly discourses that must have taken place in gentle homes of the nineteenth century in well-off families in our motherland, the UK. Maybe my mind is filled with the television stories from that time period. Sorry I could not help you more, but I do not give up that easily. I shall pursue other outlets tomorrow at work, and for the next few weeks, until I get some answers. Trust me to do my best."

With that Robert picked up his briefcase and headed to the door. Once outside, he got into his little Mini Cooper. The old couple stood in the doorway. They smiled and waved at the dapper little man from the university, still striving away in his world at the library archives.

Robert's email to Les a day later read as follows:

> These documents and accompanied onyx blocks were completely unknown to any of the planet's organizations and societies. It was difficult to get an opinion other than the parcel must remain in the hands to whom it was addressed. There is no knowledge of these items, but it is thought that similar artifacts might have been seen in antiquity. However, such information is speculative from those who wanted to assist me.
>
> My searches of the current ancient history collective were to see whether there was a hint of similar artifacts known to a select few who had such an interest or

knowledge over the ages. Even these peripheral sources had no knowledge or documentation that could be shared. My take is that this unusual box of oddities was given to you to search out something unusual in the evolution of humankind. Les, maybe you can use this enigma in one of your novels. If after your searches all is left to speculation, or even if it was intended to be noted as a historical fact, confusion and all associated knowledge collected to date may be of literary interest.

One of my facetious contacts suggested that it was the intention of unknown forces that only an unlikely mediocre scholar and his scientific wife should have this doubtful privilege. No one else on planet Earth will see or get the chance to interpret or learn from these documents and artifacts. There appeared to be a complete shutdown of all information with regard to the items. Les, I ask myself why.

This response puzzled this couple greatly for Robert was a trusted individual and it now appeared to be a conspiracy of silence. Les and Alice were willing to donate the items to any institution that Robert suggested, but there were no takers.

As to why one individual was chosen to undertake this task and why such an insignificant couple was unanswerable. Les spoke quietly to his spouse, "You know, Love, I shall tackle this as I have done in the past, when publishing my technical articles in the lab many years ago. I shall screen out the scientific knowledge from the translations of Lucretius to the Greek philosophers and seek the translation of the Sanskrit texts. That will be the beginning of my literature search. I would like you to assist me, Love."

"Did you for one minute think you could leave me out? Of course I shall do the digging into the literature and will mine for relevant information. If possible, I shall get the other translations. It should keep us old farts occupied for some time. After all, what is so important in our lives right now? Yes, we will have some fun on this project, eh!" Alice gaily replied.

Still thinking out aloud, the old author caught the gist of a game at hand with his wife, his friend and partner for six decades. He continued, "I shall prepare the experimental design, which will give a logical sequence of steps that should lead to finding answers. What do you think?"

Alice replied, going about her domestic chores, "Well, it worked for you in the past, so I do not see why it will not serve you now. Go for it. The worst that can come out of all that sweat is knowledge and fun while reading the background literature. You seem to love that form of purgatory. I shall continue to watch the television documentaries and fall asleep as I usually do—of course only after I have done all the slog work. Let us have some fun."

A brief silence followed, which was suddenly broken as Alice carried on in a more introspective tone: "Do you really want to know what these artifacts mean or what message they may contain? Just a thought."

"Well, yes, in fact. Both! Do you not want to know?"

Alice paused before speaking. "Sometimes we think we would like to know details of many events and happenings from one point of view. However, in the spirit of the moment, it would just be nice to know. On the other hand, would these findings make my mind uncomfortable? Would knowing misdirect my calm spiritual peace, which has been a happy part of our retirement? There are a lot of things I would not want to know if my peace of mind were to be disturbed."

Les replied, "I understand that outlook, but, my dear, we were good scientists in our day. Of course we did not break any frontiers of science. All we did was to perform tests that gave physicians a chance to come to a diagnosis of an illness. In my case, it was if there was an infection backed by abnormal hematological lab results. Remember, we studied for decades after grammar school and have read dozens of journals, and that broadened our knowledge so we could do our jobs better. We also taught students the practical aspects of theory, and we wrote papers on case histories. I gave lots of lectures internally in the health centre and worldwide in our heyday, and you were with me many times, if I do recall. Amidst all of this we collected advanced degrees."

Alice said, "Oh yes, I understand, but you had more academic training, so I suppose you delved deeper than I did into your discipline. To be truthful, at this stage of our lives, while it would be nice to know things, if it has any bad effect on our lives, it will not be worth it."

# CHAPTER 3

# Aged Misunderstanding and Curiosity of Humans

Les said to his wife, "While I understand all you have said, you know it is not in my nature to give up an enquiry or to leave uncertain scientific facts alone. I become as the proverbial dog with a bone; it torments my mind until I get some type of an answer. Then I put it out of mind and forget it. You know that."

Alice replied, "Oh, I do understand! And to be truthful, you have had quite a measure of success even after retirement, or rather when you decided to retire. I measure success after our careers by income, and you have been able to bring income that has seen us do much more than others who have played their lives overly protected. For that I am thankful. My problem is that you do not seem to have an off switch."

Les said, "Oh, but I do, and that could happen at any time. It is called death. That will turn me off completely and keep me silent permanently."

"Now you are being supercilious and silly. You know what I mean," Alice said. "On the other hand"—she giggled— "it is the answer to all of life's silliness, isn't it?"

After a long pause, the old couple sat down in their comfortable old office, empty tea mugs on the crowded desks. Alice was looking at her iPad, now at rest, just showing the icons, and the old man was staring through his window over his old desktop computer. He was looking at the same scenery that he had seen for the better part of six decades, but was he seeing the scenery at all?

Alice said to him, "Sometimes I think we do not always understand each other's outlook or point of view when we discuss anything. I stay quiet, but I know that you do not believe what we have discussed from my viewpoint. Your mind looks at things differently. While none of what we discuss has much to do with our quality of life, there is no risk to any of our little undertakings. I just do not know."

Les answered, "To be truthful, it is my curiosity that is deeply ingrained in my makeup that few seem to understand. Regardless of how many times I have proven my point of view, there is still no confidence that I will be able to achieve a good ending. I have learnt over my lifetime, from the time I was a boy making a plane of two small pieces of wood nailed together in a $T$ shape. On its main shape I placed small handmade U-shaped clips made of chicken wire. On a length of copper wire that I found under the new lamppost in the street, after the electricians had finished their work, I joined the pieces together and stretched the wire from the back porch to the garage, well over thirty feet away.

"I let fly my plane downwards, but it rolled upside down. I quietly worked to place balances on the wings. Using the coarse thread from my mother's sewing machine, I could let fly my plane downwards. Remaining in one position, I could pull it towards my location, which was the high part of the porch, and repeat the process. My cousin came over and asked, 'Can I have a go at flying your plane?' I let him have it, but he was laughing at my earlier attempts. The interest in the plane did not last, but the little structure remained for others to fly it. Many of our street friends appeared to get some joy just watching the little rough toy sail downwards.

"That same summer—actually it was the next day—I rescued six old broom handles from a garbage heap, brought them home on the bus and began to clean them and make 'stumps' for our little cricket club. No one said anything of the six new stumps that appeared. Cricket occupied our young lives for many years. The old stumps made of broom handles lived again, but I never knew when they disappeared or who took them away. By that time, I had moved on to college, and that took all my energies."

Alice said, "Suppose we find out what the manuscript reveals and what the runes on the onyx blocks mean. Then what? At our age, no one listens to us. Even if it is earth-shattering, who would want to know what we two geriatrics have discovered? Whom would you send it to, since no one was interested when Robert asked around? You saw the effect it had on Robert at the university. He must now think of us or you as a halfwit. He would not send it to any authority for fear of being accused of crying wolf."

Les replied, "When you put it that way, you are quite correct, Love. But I do trust Robert, so do not be too harsh on him. He is an honest man."

Alice said, "Once you understand that sequence of possibilities and are willing to accept all that it implies, know that neither fame nor fortune will be your payment. Now, you can have some fun uncovering the truths of these artifacts. I will assist you as much as you need and will always be at your side."

"Alice, my love, I knew that you would want to be involved. There is an inherent curiosity in a scientific mind. It is like the bait on the hook of a fishing line. It calls even when there is danger, and you still have it even when you have tried to bury it, ha ha! Thanks for the offer. You can begin with the literature search list I placed on your desk."

# SECTION II

Aliens outside the Earth's solar system have been monitoring this segment of the cosmos for generations. What happened when one of their ancient travellers found Earth 14 million years ago? His journals were reviewed by a new generation of travellers from the planet Sig.

# CHAPTER 4

# Somewhere in Deep Space

"Well, our mission is to follow up on an experiment designed by our ancestors in this solar system four generations ago. It began on this planet that is covered in water, and it appears to have been so for the last one and a half million Earth years. It is a nice planet, appearing blue to azure in colour. It has a balanced atmosphere that has allowed both zoological and botanical life forms to exist and prosper," the Commander stated in a matter-of-fact tone.

First Officer of Demographics and Planetary Settlements stated, "Well, Sir, it is a bit of a cold file really. I make this suggestion after clearing up the backlog of unfinished cosmic exploitations and experiments in this quadrant of our planetary exploration. This file popped up as unfinished, and the small lights mean it cannot be denied. As we are in this vicinity, it is our duty, rather our responsibility, to provide a final report and to close off all outstanding experiments, whether or not they are successful. Our files require conclusions after determining whether this was a worthwhile endeavour on our ancient pioneer commander's part. He may have made decisions on behalf of the senate on planet Sig."

"Bloody cold file! Man, this planet must have been seeded by our previous ancestors around a light year ago. Have the details ready for me in my quarters. Make yourself available over the next few hours to answer any questions I may have in understanding what our ancients have done," came the terse response from Commander Caden of the giant spaceship *Reja*.

"I have summarized the details of their research and their plans to have a reliable workforce develop and live here. The details of genetic insertion and the use of primitive traits and a structured leadership were all that was needed. If you really would like to see the recorded details of the plans as well as the procedures used, I could have these ready, but it will take a little time. I shall be around working on other files, Sir, and will make myself available on this project," responded the gentle first officer Glen.

With that brief discussion, Commander Caden of the spaceship *Reja* went off to his suite of rooms to review his files. He went straight to his desk and opened the files from the chip, which lit up his desk as he approached. He saw a photo of the old commander of planet Sig who had set the goal of exploring the universe in search of similar life forms. He knew the details of this historical decision that set the mission for his race, the Sigs. Such details were taught to every offspring in the first year of their development and during their advanced training.

Commander Caden sat back, looking at the brightly lit screen, and his mind was cast back to his early beginnings when he, amongst other siblings, had spoken up that he wanted to spend his life exploring the outer cosmos. He vowed that it would be his life's commitment. He had read up and been educated on all that was needed by his planet in those early days. In the back of his mind, he kept his personal goal alive by seeking out knowledge on his own. He wanted to know all that was needed to become a commander of a ship of planet Sig.

His only family comprised fellow students, and his tutors who were living beings; the robots did most of the tutoring. The Sigs were an advanced race of primate beings that had evolved rapidly with an understanding that they were the chosen in the universe. They had built a civilization that did not have wars or want for survival necessities. Each one of the planet's inhabitants was equal in that they never knew want of anything to survive. Everything that was necessary for their growth and maintenance of their health, including food and sanitation, was installed early in their evolution.

What continued to fire the imagination of the intellectual leadership chosen by the masses, for universal communication allowed every citizen to vote, was the goal of seeking a family in the cosmos. The leadership set the goal of finding a primate species similar to themselves. They wished to develop relationships to further enhance their own culture and society. First, the needs of the population and what was good for keeping their planet viable indefinitely were secured with every citizen contributing to the universal welfare.

The development of the Sigs' planet and its zoological selection led to a race of advanced evolved individuals to form the first utopian society in the cosmos. The Commander remembered his early years studying the philosophers of old, who expressed that there was nothing else in the cosmos but atoms and empty space. All the rest was the imagination with no limit for there was only emptiness.

Commander Caden quietly wondered why his race did not have to struggle against the elements of nature or with the different races of beings, as there were different physical attributes. In many such tribes, enlarged ears, large buboes under the armpits that enhanced immunity, and three-digit protrusions at the end of their hands and feet were commonplace.

Their planet had many animals and flying life forms that all seemed to look after themselves, finding what was needed to keep themselves healthy and able to reproduce within the massive surrounding forests and other ecosystems. Caden's race never found the need to eat flesh because the botanical life forms of trees and plants provided all they needed for a healthy survival. Later on their scientists concentrated these nutritional food products into a small pill to be taken daily by every citizen on Sig. This development allowed the Sigs to travel without need for bulky food storage.

After rapidly exploring their own environment, during which they mapped the physical industrial resources, they found plentiful inorganic deposits that allowed them to build a huge armada of flying spaceships that took them to different sections throughout the cosmos.

Development of a transport system on their planet's surface led to development of vehicles that did not congest land space. They used the space above the planet to cover vast distances rapidly. The senate was made up of different elected clans who openly answered all questions. However, for the educated mind there was one philosophical question. The unknown factor that was on every citizen's mind was why they had life so easy. Who was it that designed their race and influenced their rapid development through a relatively short evolution? Of more importance, why had this happened? What was the reason and purpose?

Caden spoke out loud to himself: "My old tutors told me that there had to be a supernatural force they did not know of, a benign Creator or a God who quietly guided them to the society they had become." He smiled and stood up, looking through the window at the darkness outside his ship that was travelling at the speed of light.

Yes. This type of thinking was done quietly by a few of his teaching masters. He knew of a few who had many such outlandish thoughts and had chosen to live away from active society. They chose to live in isolation—a hermit's life—without the need for physical comforts.

Caden smiled to himself. "One of these was my aged scholarly tutor who was learned in many dialects and made the learning of them easy for all students and for himself. He had told me that isolation and self-denial of physical comfort took him to a state of deep spirituality. In that state, he said, he could mentally travel into outer space without leaving the planet."

Caden continued, "I enquired why he wanted such a remote place to mentally comfort himself."

He remembered the wry smile on the old bearded face. "You see, my clever student, it is a form of addiction open to a few. Self-denial opens up when there is physical suppression, which is expressed in mental strength of thought. When the mind dominates our being, there is a satiation that produces pure thought, where nothing is unattainable with regard to either physical or mental needs," explained Caden's spiritual father Michael, whom the former trusted implicitly.

Commander Caden did spend some time with his spiritual father to try to understand himself, unknowing at the time why he was searching; invariably it was to verify what he really wanted to spend his life doing. He was now doing exactly what he had prepared all his life to do. He must stop fussing at what was done a million light years earlier and try to understand the thinking in that ancient period. At the same time, there was a fascination with the old masters of yesteryear who met conditions that he could never hope to discover now, so many light years later. His future travelling the cosmos, like everything else in life, never remained the same. Change was the universal constant. That much he had learned from his own experience.

Caden reviewed his ancestor's experimental design from his early plans onwards.

"Verbal request: Commander Caden of the spaceship *Reja*. Open records." Video records opened of an old communication recording. He heard the following:

"My name is Commander Sitla of planet Sig on a journey to find a life form, preferably a primate similar to our species. My mandate is very broad in scope for we are an advanced scientific race. After a light year exploring the universe, we have found no civilized race similar to us. Now that I have aged rapidly, we are alone after many light years of travelling, by hundreds of my predecessors, throughout the cosmos."

The recording continued, "There have been planets with sun-like stars, many of which appear capable of supporting biological life in different solar systems. To date, we have found none with a biological system or life forms similar to us. Indeed, only microbes have been isolated by our on-board laboratories. There were a few planets that had a basic plant/botanical system but were still evolving; it would take many centuries before mature forests would have grown. Others had vast amounts of liquid methane we collected under extreme conditions which we have used for fuel in our backup systems.

"One thing is definite: there are large amounts of water on many planets, but few planets with any evolved zoological or botanical life forms except for primitive algae.

"We are a long-lived race. For purposes of comparison, we have been exploring at the edge of the Milky Way. It is where we found a small solar system with a twenty-four-hour period of time when each planet rotates around the sun star, so that one-half of the planet experiences a time of bright light while the other half experiences darkness. These planets remain in a permanent orbit around the Sun. They all appear to have equal daylight and darkness, which I chose to call a day and night period. Our huge exploration and scientific collection spaceship has been placed into a regular orbit around the Sun, similar to that of the other, lifeless planets.

"We found a time period of three hundred and sixty-five days to be a good way to record the time of a biological being's life span from birth to death on the one blue planet with primitive life forms of both botanical and zoological variety. We called this completed cycle after many of the local time periods, an annum.

"We, in comparison, have a life span of one thousand or more anni. We chose the third planet, which had significant amounts of water and land with forests where life forms in both the saltwater seas and on land appeared to be rapidly, relatively speaking, undergoing an evolutionary phase that could be studied by simple observation and then recorded to be later analyzed. It was an ideal scientific in vivo experiment, not of our scientific biased design.

"There was a spiritual aspect that was completely fascinating to all our scientists, who detected it by observing the primates. I held regular daily meetings with the whole crew. These and the meetings held by our scientists ensured that the whole crew knew the results of our findings. The enthusiasm shown by our professionals, all second generation, born on our ship, was wonderful to behold. It is here that I thought the end of our search should take place."

# CHAPTER 5

# Period of Exploration and Abstracted Decisions

### Decision 1

The files of Commander Sitla continued:

"We looked and explored the planet with a view to documenting all aspects of its mineral deposits and its biomes. To this task, I placed our finest officer, Hodge, to explore and list all mineral deposits. We were never to take away any of the mineral wealth. Our mandate was to explore, not to remove any of, the planet's assets. We found much that was worthy as the planet had huge deposits of carbon-based elements, mineral deposits in large amounts as hard beams binding the formations of the solid structure of the rocky earth, and massive amounts of iron ore.

"Hodge reported that many large meteorites had bombarded the planet, depositing large amounts of water and minerals and with its force, restructuring the physical makeup of this little planet. At the end of his survey, using our advanced technology, Hodge completed the whole physical makeup of this little planet. His report can be found under the heading of 'Mineralogy, the Solar System at the End of the Stream of Stars.'"

## Decision 2

"This was more difficult because, using the same tools within our powerful ship, we sent our biological experts to use their skills in investigating the planet zoological and botanical life forms. Our experts were not to trap or destroy any of the botanical makeup. However, they were to seek out those items that were nutritional to the animals on the planet. Our zoologists had a similar mandate to map every animal from the microscopic to the largest life forms found on the surface of the planet, including the vast freshwater bodies. They were each to be studied, analyzed, and researched as to their respective contribution to the ecosystem. The same had to be done in the deep salty oceans, and while that posed severe difficulties, it made for great excitement. Our scientists who were older, and those Sigs who were born and had grown up in these professions on our ship, reveled in their excitement.

"The practical uses of our technology, along with the development of testing protocols and new tools, created an excitement among our massive crew that took on a life of its own. At sessions after our meals, all the teams present gave internal lectures throughout the ship on their findings. Our senior scientists explained what had been found and put forward theories on the laws governing physics, chemistry, microbiology and biology, as well as the basics of anthropology, all in relation to primate development.

"Predicting the evolutionary trend was more challenging, and for many on this planet, it took years to test hypotheses and plan their own disciplines' study. The data collected led our most experienced scientists to produce hypotheses that were proven in the field for the younger, less experienced crew members.

"Let the records show that as commander of our ship, I was totally enamored with the whole massive study we had undertaken. I got to rest at this interlude for the data had grown to such a volume, it was becoming difficult for our computers to analyze. We needed to develop improved technology to analyze the massive data collected from the fieldwork.

"Duplication of all the ship's resources had been completed as requested."

## Commander Sitla Outlined the Future to His Fellow Officers

"My officers, there are now three generations of Sigs on our ship. I have deliberately set this planet as a homeland for all crew mates, especially those who have grown old and may wish to settle down on a hard surface rather than a flying spaceship. Yes, we shall never see planet Sig again, and since there are no other beings like us, it is time to create a livable environment to end our days and years of space travel across the cosmos. This planet is about the best that we have found to date. It has all that is necessary for a primate life form like us."

There was a pause in the recording.

"For this to happen, it will be necessary for us to intercede using our expertise in the biological sciences, using the skills of our geneticists and molecular biologists, and using the soft sciences. There were no rules governing the end of life when we could no longer pursue our goal because of our ageing ship's expended expertise in aspects of advanced medicine given to me as commander. So I chose to use my influence and the knowledge of our crew to examine all non-primate life forms on this humanoid world. In fact, I simply stated that I decided to seek out a primate similar to us, or close to us in biology, and try to integrate as much as was possible.

"If any civilization was found unlike us in physical image, or one that was aggressive, we were to avoid those life forms. Angry, hateful and warlike habitations would be imported into our people's lives should we try to befriend such civilizations."

He paused again.

"I bring these matters up because I believe that while our ship is able to service us for a few more centuries of 'local time,' we should look for another home in which to spend our final days. To attempt returning to our home planet, Sig, would cause frustration of the worst kind because many of the present generation would not be the ones arriving but two generations later. Anyway, the more I think of this prospect, the more I see it has no merit. For what knowledge would our third generation bring to Sig that was of value?

"I ask that we begin a massive study of the uninhabited planet that was created for a species such as ourselves. Since I will not ask our crew to settle down on this unknown planet, it would also be unfair for us to usurp a gentle biological garden and make it in our image. We do not have the monopoly on what is right or wrong. Regardless of Sig's history, it does not hold sway in the deep cosmos.

"Since I have lived half a lifetime on board, there is a need to refurbish our supplies of fresh water and to secure new and varied botanical plants for our dietary needs. Therefore, these are two major goals I would like to set in motion immediately. My next task is a reassignment of all leadership positions on the ship. In fact, amongst these leaders my recommendation is that there be a doubling of individuals for each of these positions. We need a mirror image of each and every one of us through an applied apprenticeship in training our youth. If that means increasing our number of offspring, then so be it. Next, using our skills of choosing the best individuals, after training, half of these duplicates will be put into a state of prolonged stasis and incubation for ten of our lifetimes.

"The second goal is to maintain all botanical life forms from Sig in continuous culture, but a small sample should be transplanted on the planet below. At the same time, if there are useful botanical plants on that blue planet below us that could be of use to our civilization on the ship, they are to be studied and evaluated as to their usefulness to us. If proven to be an asset to us on board, we should include them in our herbarium. Great care must be taken when introducing new biological samples from an alien planet into our strictly controlled herbarium.

"With zoological life forms, I should like a complete report first from our anthropologists who have been studying these primates that have similar physical features to ours. Similarly, I would like a report from our archaeologists showing how these primates are evolving and where they hibernate during inclement weather or when under attack by another tribe. Our geneticists will carry out a complete analysis and mapping of those species that have the potential traits leading to a civilized and dominant species on this planet.

"Let there be a complete record of all activities as we make planetary adjustments to accommodate one stable primate life form. Hopefully this species will evolve to become the owners of this planet. Over time, and when the occasion is correct, they will take their place in the cosmos. I strongly suggest that that we leave clues in stone structures and in their archeological deposits. The purpose for this recommendation is that this species may set out into space in the future. It is my hope that one day they may find planet Sig, where they would be accepted by our senate.

"Officers and subcommanders, these are my wishes. We have done what was expected of us when we started out on this search of the cosmos. A reality check reveals that were we to set out now for planet Sig, it would take about three to five generations before reaching home. That would be unfair to all those who would die on the return journey. It is better to engage in a planned enterprise that could have far-reaching consequences.

"I will remain as the last commander from planet Sig on this starship while this major work is undertaken. The next commander will have benefited from my training here on board, and that individual will be placed into stasis to be awakened at my death. We must combine our efforts to ensure there will be complete understanding of this planetary experiment and its goals. We will have given our civilization a worthy cosmic companion sometime in the future."

There was yet another pause.

"There are cosmic changes that must be compensated for. As our charts and measurements have indicated, the cosmos is expanding rapidly, so all planets are drifting farther apart. We have in our possession charts and records that should guide future generations back to our home planet. However, on leaving planet Sig, it was never the expectation that any commander and his ship should ever return, especially if no civilization similar to that of Sig was never found.

"All our biological requirements, our professional scientists, and our technologies old and new must be duplicated. I now ask our engineers to build a ship similar to this giant on which we live, deep in space away from where we are currently in orbit. It must be made with the finest materials and new alloy combinations from the surrounding planets, the exception being the planet we are studying below us. None of its resources should be touched, mined or exploited in any way.

"I would first like to have the anthropological plan, followed by a complete report in one year's time as measured in this solar system. The report and accompanying suggestions should be completed with a hypothesis on how genetic intervention in a chosen primate species would cause it to evolve into a civilized species capable of learning to conquer the obstacles in exploiting the power of the cosmos. In time, they will be able to head in the direction from which we came. We will require these plans as soon as they become available.

"I have chosen the leader in charge of the anthropological exploration to be Anneg, a professor of great repute. She was involved in the later exploration of planet Sig and contributed many theories as to how our civilization originated. Professor Anneg, please pick your team and make it fewer than two hundred scientists and workers. Please use the powerful resources of this ship to scan significant sites of interest. I ask, however, that none of the bones or skulls of the native population be disrupted or removed. They must remain in situ. This means that your studies should be done on-site. Some of your theories may include a degree of conjecture, so that would be acceptable."

After another pause, the Commander continued: "Next, the leader of the archaeological site will be Loug of the museums of Sig. Loug, you will also choose a team, but no more than one hundred scientists and technical workers. Your task, however, seeing as this planet does not appear to have any worthwhile buildings on its surface, is to verify there are no building artifacts on the planet, and that includes caves used by the inhabitants for whatever reasons. However, if there are etchings, paintings or basic writing, they are to be recorded in the context of your discipline for our files.

"Neither must they be removed nor moulds made from them, and only a pictorial record will be required for our records. There is, however, a greater task that I desire, and that is for you to develop clues that would denote from whence we came, showing the quadrant and location of planet Sig in the cosmos. Secondly, let the indigenes or native population look forward to our return sometime in the future. Please have a plan on how you may accomplish this task."

Almost immediately, there was a rapid response from Anneg, asking the commander and his group of advisors to review the basic outline of her experimental design based on his instructions. Commander Sitla was not one to be easily caught by surprise, but after many years of travelling across the cosmos and taking measurements from within the ship's powerful sensors, the crew wanted real pioneer assignments. Such enthusiasm revealed their pent-up need to explore further in the field, and this planetary system seemed to provide that opportunity.

These practical assignments were the cause for a massive professional breakthrough for thousands of crew members. The ships' computers recorded and analyzed the outline of the tasks desired, but robots did the work. The programmed robots crunched the data, applying all new information obtained by the myriad of scanners focused on the blue planet. From such data, they produced the experimental design for the individual professional in charge.

Anneg's plan was simple and is summarized as follows:

1.  To search for a primate that has the potential to evolve rapidly with some assistance of genetic enhancement.
2.  To examine the geological terrain and its role in the biological environment, determining how it plays a role in advancing one hominid.
3.  The physical configuration of Sigs entail two upper and two lower appendages with an upright stance and a head with a brain capable of developing and storing information. Towards this end, the lead hand should study the role of savannah in the prehistory of this planet, recording and listing animals common to this ecosystem.
4.  Focus on primates and see what archaeological sites have been left intact for the team to record, study and interpret.
5.  Examine the formation of livable sites that would outline the planet's hominid prehistory.
6.  Try to interpret the prehistory of all primates and hominids on the planet.
7.  With regard to primate origins, begin to examine the housing used by the early life forms we are interested in, such as burrows in the ground and nests in trees and in high mountain caves. Seek, through observation of a select group that represents the primate under study, the following:

    a.  Presence of claws and/or a prehensile thumb with smaller digits at the end of the upper limb.

b. Whether this primate is able to see in colour, for which a complex cortex is vital. This will be ascertained in a living being using scanning equipment.

c. The formation of traits such as insecurity, emotion and inhibition, which are essential to any primate in that these show the ability to choose—the power of choice. This is trait is essential for survival of the species, and it is one that brings about learning through practice and decision making.

# CHAPTER 6

# Wisdom of a Leader

As Commander Caden read and absorbed details from the files of his ancient counterpart Commander Sitla, separated by time measured in light years, he began to analyze the decisions made by the historic commander. Mumbling to himself, he said, "Sitla knew at the time he would never see his home planet, Sig, again. He decided to create a hominid population that had all the native skills for survival on this evolving planet. By his interruption or interceding, he produced a race that would one day, he hoped, find our old planet, Sig. That would remove the feeling of being alone in the cosmos.

"*Laudable indeed!*" he barked out in his own room. "Leadership is not an easy task.

"These primate beings, Sitla learned from his anthropologist, would each have the capability to evolve into a 'better' individual from his and his co-leader's perspective. The concept of 'better' never seemed to have been discussed. Just as well, as it would have opened up a discussion leading to an ascribed philosophy and ethical behaviour and would bias abstraction.

"*Interesting.*

"Commander Sitla's alternative plan should there be a catastrophic failure, for which he would take full responsibility, was to have a new ship ready to continue Sig's mission indefinitely into the future. It would be up to a new commander to decide and take the initiative to return to Sig, even if it would take three or more generations to find his or her way home. The question he had toyed with for many years was, to what avail should he seek to return, only to report on their failure in finding another cosmic population as described by Sig leadership? There was no merit in that decision as far as he was concerned." *An abstraction.*

## Examination of a New Philosophy

"Commander Sitla observed that the cosmos created many planets and that there was a wealth of resources for his/our species or any other to exploit and to develop. After all, that is what our species did when they used their own planet's mineral and biological wealth to evolve rapidly, relative to the birth of their planet. In Sitla's mind, he would help the cosmos since he was from a chosen race of primates. They had the opportunity to grow into something more from their own primitive existence. Surely that was a gift to be shared. After many light years of travel, his own ship's population had grown." *Deduction.*

"Commander Sitla visited a number of dead but mineral-rich planets and exploited those resources to extend the size of his ship. He and his crew were now utilizing new sources of energy that were more efficient and in plentiful supply." *A clever decision made by a leader and his team.*

"Of course, the population on the ship had been taught from an early age by programmed tutor robots that were also updating their knowledge base. They were learning from the exploits and scientific changes made in fuel and production of new alloys. Such activities produced a quantum increase in scientific knowledge. Sitla would use this combined power of knowledge and the mandate of his leadership to generate a race that had the potential to evolve into a capable being."

"After all," Commander Caden muttered into the recording of his files, "who is to know that this was not our unwritten mandate for our creation on Sig?"

*Regard for wisdom of a past leader. Deductions*—just a few, made by Commander Sitla:

"Well, this file should cover any misperception, hint or clue as to why we were created and, to some degree, compensate for the lack of information as to how the majestic cosmos began and developed into such a miraculous creation. Sig's wisdom in our age is to refute the idea of any superbeing or designer that controlled the great power that we witnessed from our travels through the cosmos and about which we have gained a little understanding.

"I have asked myself repeatedly over my long lifetime why the perception of spirituality has been deliberately missed in our education and philosophy. There is an inherent divinity that calls for the concept of a Creator. The co-leadership and I, along with our brain trust team, continue to remain away from the day-to-day activity of the professional teams. However, when we are alone, I make my thoughts known to them just as an idea. From these basic suggestions, intellectual freedom was offered to the full crew to think more broadly outside our academic limitations.

"This group formed a hypothesis of their own about cogitation from a philosophical perspective of a greater power than the cosmos, in fact, the power of one that directs physical formations through a range of powers, many of which we are still unaware of, such as gravity. In fact, they began their own analogy by expanding the concept of the cosmos and taking a broader and more expansive view on the philosophy behind the leadership of the Sig decision to set in motion the search for similar civilizations.

"Even when we decided to explore this smaller solar system, rich in mineral wealth and being located as the third planet from its star, there was a blue tinge. Scanners confirmed there were massive amounts of water covering well over two-thirds of its surface. This observation was shown to the whole crew throughout the ship. There was silence. My ship's crew had observed, recorded and scientifically studied wonderful sights in the absence of sound. They had gained different experiences as we travelled through darkness over many light years.

Their enthusiasm for studying exploding suns undergoing supernova, and now finding this real garden of a planet that had no technological primate, overwhelmed their minds. These were ship-born Sigs. They only knew the spaceship as their planet. Even with all the tutoring on the topic of their home planet, they only knew the giant metal monster *Reja* as their home. The pressure for me to let them know that there was a real planet base on which we could survive with other natural bioforms was overwhelming. That was when I was approached by the team."

*The team—an opinion:* the value of a brain trust for discussion only.

"Honorable Commander, I am one of the seers of the brain trust on this ship. We were entrusted with knowledge no others have on this ship because of our genetic makeup, which has endowed us with a longer life span than on our home world. As a result, like you, I am one of the original crew members. Our accumulated knowledge is stored in *Reja's* computers. Our sect had taken a vow of non-interference to be upheld throughout the journey. Our task was to dispassionately look at all that was experienced and to learn but also to adapt our opinions to assist our commander when asked.

"Our code: We may only give our opinions and guidance when we are asked to do so by the commander of this mighty ship. The leaders of Sig knew that there was a high probability that we would not find a similar civilization to ours.

"The leaders believed that all that was good in our civilization and our society would survive among the crew to their benefit. They also felt that at some time, after many light years of experience, the ship would gradually deteriorate and would no longer be a viable entity. It was felt the commander would make the decision to find a new home for the crew, but this was but one among other worthwhile suggestions. They envisaged there would be a chosen planet where the ship would land and form a colony, a new Sig. These were the private concerns of our leaders when we left. Our aged elders were carrying out all that had been part of the mission of Sig, set many light years earlier.

"With knowledge comes wisdom, and the thought of many crews who were surveying the cosmos and never returning home must have pricked the conscience of the Sig leadership.

"We, the chosen brain trust, believe that when you brought up this idea, it must have come to you from the cosmos itself. We now feel that you should execute your detailed plans from your leadership perspective. We particularly like the backup system of a new ship, even though our ship is still worthwhile and sturdy and could continue for many light years into the future.

"Your plan for a new civilization of our own design, having basic genetic enhancements, is a good one. However, there is a proviso that if indeed there is a worthwhile race on the third planet that could eventually evolve to be a civilization in its own right, it should be left alone. There should be no interference on our part. However, using our technology, we could teach through our leadership by rendering tasks that such a race would follow. In mimicking or copying tasks that we could show them, they would learn—an apprenticeship, so to speak.

"What must be avoided at all costs is that they must never become reliant on us and our technological power. Indeed, none of our technology should be shared at this stage of their primitive evolution. Of course, we should use our skills and technology to accomplish those building tasks as outlined by the archaeologists in their report. They have found primitive drawings of hunting scenes, done by primates living together in caves and underground habitats. They had left handprints and drawings of their lives. Why they did this has not been successfully interpreted at this time by our teams.

"The varied races on this planet called Earth found food from their surroundings on land and in the water. The most successful primates appear to thrive because of a high-protein diet. They are eating the zoological life forms, which provides nutrition of protein, carbohydrates and fats. We have watched them hunt, kill and eat the flesh of their herbivores, and in one tribe we saw them actually eating one of their own species. As a result, these early primates have survived different climatic conditions, especially in the northern parts of the planet.

"Fact: They learned to follow herds of animals for their food, thus maintaining their health and keeping the basic family unit together as it grew. Whether by plan, by instinct or because of changes in climate, they adapted with the food sources available and survived. It may appear that much of what they do is instinctual at this stage in their evolution, but is there an underlying intelligence?

"Their prehistory is very interesting according to our anthropologists' reports. From their early prehominid days, they left the trees while other primates continued an arboreal existence. Hence they had intelligence and were advanced. They then spread out across the savannahs in search of food, following herds of herbivores. They travelled, leaving their surroundings and creating a lifestyle that allowed them to experience new vistas and experiences when travelling on their hunts.

"Later on, many of these ambulatory primates that were constantly travelling came to the great oceans of water. They travelled around its shorelines, which allowed them and their followers to move away from the continental forested and savannah surroundings. As they travelled the coastline, they learned to catch and eat aquatic animals, allowing for a more varied diet. This meant new tools, which they might have copied from the coastline brethren, were developed. Archaeological evidence shows they also made new weapons using slate pieces and sharp stones attached to long rods to form spears and fish hooks, all killing tools, which shows a primal ability to gain and use knowledge as an advanced species.

"As they travelled, they lived beside the great saltwater oceans. Food was plentiful along these shores. Soon there were breakaway groups. Some went to the northern parts of the planet, others to the east and some to the southwest.

"As a result, they left no evidence of permanent structures in which they lived. However, eating around the fireside, discarding the bones of animals, fish and birds, along with broken pottery, would become markers in a great puzzle for future generations to unravel. We have evidence from their teeth found in skulls, which reveal their different diets. For meat eaters, their teeth had sharp points, better for tearing flesh.

"The vegetation eaters had smaller front teeth but larger back teeth used for grinding their food of nuts and seeds. They had lost their reliance of using all four limbs to move around in favour of bipedalism. The upper appendages became more tactile and were used to make tools from the wealth of raw materials readily available in their surroundings.

"It was only a matter of time before they began to use the raw coal formed from aged trees buried under pressure from tectonic upheavals. This natural process brought about by planetary upheavals allowed formation of seams of coal. The burning of wood and now of coal for heat are indicators of an evolving species. Over time there has been an increase in brain size as a result of meat eating. At least these are the abstractions we made.

"Through their migrations, there has been a change in bone structure that correlates with different climatic and geographic locations. Examination of the skulls of those that went farther north and experienced severe colder climate changes revealed an increase in skeletal mass. Similar but different changes were observed in those skulls isolated under warm climatic conditions. Geologically there appeared to be large ice sheets that came down from the North Pole to cover half the great northern oceans. This drove the animals south and left few species capable of living in the frozen waters of the new arctic regions of the planet.

"The note of importance is that many hominids and other animal herds were capable of travelling across the ice plates and snow. When the ice receded, they found themselves in new territories. They found food plentiful and untouched resources, and better living beckoned. As more information comes in from our exploratory scientific crews and teams, we shall do the analysis and keep you informed, Commander."

# CHAPTER 7

# Genetics, Power and Leadership

## Anthropological Observations

"The fact that a bigger, or rather a more complicated, brain evolved as a result of hunting and eating animal flesh. The activity stimulated in this primitive hominid was the acceptable trait of killing for food but also the killing of each other. The example cited: if two hunters from different territories were stalking the same game and one killed the animal, it would not be a stretch of the imagination that the loser would attempt to kill the victor to get at the game. The analogy is well-founded because the family unit had become a reality, along with the force of providing food and protection. Consequently, there was a longer infant dependency, which fell to the female, who looked after the protection and nurturing of the next generation."

## More Observations

The report continues: "As a result, the roles of the male and female became obvious. The female was the homemaker, the protector of the new generation and the one who gave a mixed diet to the family. The male became the physical protector from other, encroaching, more aggressive hominids and wild animals. He also had to hunt and bring in fresh meat to keep up with the needs of nutrition of the now increasingly evolving family. This dependency on the female meant that child-bearing females had become a commodity for hungry, sexually aroused males.

"Sexual availability and receptivity had become essential traits that a healthy male would want to keep for himself. That would include fighting to keep his mate. The females soon saw their power in the role as comforter in exchange for procreation. Such a process allowed for the selection of a good provider of food, shelter and protection as being worthwhile. These are a few examples that surrounded the early primates on this planet. Many of these deductions also came from observations of the animals that were plentiful and by which we were surrounded.

"The biggest, more muscled stag showed its strength and better-surviving genes by carrying bigger antlers used in fighting other males and by winning and defending his harem of females. In the more closely related ape species, the huge silverback fought off his male contenders to keep his group of females. However, some females could be enticed away by a rogue male wanderer when the old king was distracted. Genetic diversity seemed to be a natural phenomenon in all successful species.

"Female promiscuity was a stimulus causing early hominid males to keep on bringing in enough food and paying attention to the family. In this way, the female remained satisfied and lost the desire to stray. However, when the big male, because of age or physical impairment, lost his strength and ability to provide for the female, he would be turned away from his harem by younger, aggressive males. The females, on the other hand, would adjust to the replacement male that took charge of the family. Her sexual availability was provided from her experience in order to protect her young and to generate healthier offspring.

"As these advanced anthropologists began to study the field of sexuality and the prehistory of hominid love, their minds expanded. The power of these natural forces would, over time, like their own sexuality, become a normal act only for procreation with little binding power.

"Observation 1: While their observances were still in their early days and much was unknown, several theories could be abstracted and projected into the future. It was observed that love within the family unit advanced and became a source of pride amongst the male hunting society. But this might have been the beginning of homosexuality and also the taboo of incest. These changes in behaviour within a family unit manifested from the evolving traits of hominid behaviour.

"Observation 2: However, such emotional carnal powers would only have arisen because there was a need in that they brought the level of conflict and understanding to the female. She now assumed the role of balancing aggressive behaviour that was inherent in males using sexual favour. This aggressive gene, when advanced into full communities of villages, would see the use of force as one village attacked another village to take away their food stocks and their domesticated animals, also taking females for their own males.

"Comment—anthropological abstraction: The gene that depicts aggressiveness should be left untouched in our genetic manipulation and not be deleted because it is what our race of Sigs lacks. That lost gene allows us not to be aggressive because we are the only life form in the universe after several generations of Sigs had explored and searched the cosmos. Hypothetically, were we to find an aggressive race that would be unreasonable and would not deal with us in a civilized manner, what defences do we have?"

"Weapons were not necessary for our civilization," the commander spoke out. "In my suite, I have arms that could be mass-produced on our ship if the need should arise. However, we would have to learn to use them. The question remains, would we be able to kill another species? In a split moment of indecision and hesitation, we would be killed by an aggressive species."

There was a moment for the team to reflect.

"Profitability genes included one gene that protects the hominid from diseases that have the potential to kill many members of a susceptible species. A healthy immune system is a necessity in the new hybrids. To teach by demonstration and seek the ability to learn certain traits in leadership implies giving the majority in a village a reason for working together. This is what they must learn when we show them skills to use in food production and agriculture.

"As to implementing a leader to be in charge: knowledge based, a commander directive: If we arm the stronger members of a group with knowledge, such as when field grains should be planted in certain areas, then show the individual how to reap harvests, he would have the power and others would follow his leadership. Were we also to teach them the basics of judging the weather cycles as these affect the optimal time to plant and to reap, do you understand this real power?"

Commander Sitla bent his head as if to rest his weary brow.

Sitla said, "Yes, we ought to show the leader the best location where healthy plants and grasses are located in their forests. Similarly, we should explain the role of fish protein present in their seas, lakes, rivers and oceans. We should show them how to produce special crops and how to maintain a stock of seeds and cuttings that would allow continuity of agriculture as the main food sources. We should show the leader and his workers how to use water and take it to where it is needed when the weather is inclement, out of cycle. We must use all our technology to achieve these basic requirements on which they will come to depend. They will see the fruits of such labour and eventually emulate our leadership.

"There is risk in what we are undertaking. We must resolve to teach and show a new natural power that is not based on physical strength and aggression. We must separate these leaders from the workers and outline how leadership works. We must show them how to plan out the calendar for agriculture by using the direct approach through action and eventually through communication with words."

The directive of this commander on first contact with these primates continued in his notes: "The chosen leaders will be in charge to pass information to the workers. Over time, the leader will gain respect from his workers based on knowledge. For his doubting individuals, he must have extra persuasive power, which we will give to him. Begin with the basic knowledge of reading the stars in the universe to locate one's positon when travelling at nighttime. Use our location of the ship at nighttime to set a position for them next to the other two planets closest to the sun.

"Explain how their planet's atmosphere works so they can learn the basics of weather changes. Explain the necessity of using the land prudently, by studying it and accepting it as a gift from the Creator of the universe. Expand their knowledge by explaining their relationship in using all that we have taught them with regard to the growth of crops and the role of the sun as a necessity for their plants to grow."

"Remember, teachers," the Commander explained, "the role of the leader as teacher to the workers must have a benefit for him, and that may mean having more females around him, as well as lots of food that he did not plant. Sitting higher than the workers and dressing differently should show the separation between leader and followers. However, ensure that they do not promote themselves to the status of deity.

"They may think of us, after our departure, as the deity that came and showed them how to come together into communities. They will never need a deity, but when they look up at our spaceship that is currently coming around the sun close to Venus and Mercury, and the other planets of their solar system, they may think of the phenomenon as one."

Silence followed this speech by Commander Sitla. After a little while, a small voice was heard as First Officer Wren spoke up. "Commander Sitla, do you think such deception is a wise step in this experiment on such a basic being? Even after some genetic enhancement, why mislead these hybrids with the 'gift' of a supreme being? This may cause conflict in the future when their brains begin to function at an advanced level and individuals may not wish to believe, while the leaders who have benefited would continue to do so."

Sitla replied, "They have the gift of leadership, while the workers and later generations will not. This may lead to a situation of believers against non-believers. Those who obtain largesse from the leaders will have wealth, while others who have laboured over a generation will become dissatisfied with their lot. The sowing of these predictive seeds of discontent may cause chaos in the future. These beings will want choice, and if they keep that savage gene of killing in their makeup, they will select such a future by using force. Just my opinion."

"Well," said First Officer Wren, "and well thought out, if I may say so. There is little feedback from our planning committee of officers."

"We need more of this type of thinking, Officer Wren," stated old Commander Sitla. "It is time for a little intellectual fencing with the first officers involved in planning. I chose you four for the skills you have shown throughout our journey as well as for your independent thought. Now let all be free to speak as you so choose, but also let the case history commentary continue to be taped.

"My officers—Beth in charge of ethics, Officer Elle for social development, Officer Anne for genetics and Officer Karl, geology engineer—you have chosen your own teams without any guidance but your own. My task is to move the major plans forward, and you are to execute them as best you can."

First Officer Wren, emboldened by the support of his commander, answered, "That is quite so, Commander Sitla."

Officer Beth spoke up, "Commander, in all our experience of travelling under your guidance, I have …" He paused. "Maybe I may take this opportunity to speak for others here who may feel the same. On no occasion have I found any of our plans and directives discordant or aberrant in any way. Maybe from an ethics perspective, if I thought your directive was unsatisfactory, I would have spoken up on behalf of the majority of crew members and for all of us. Now you have put us in a quandary because you want feedback on what you have been assiduously thinking for many years. We have travelled many light years from Sig. I knew that we would never return when I volunteered for this search. Why do you feel the need to ask us now?"

"For the same reason, Officer Beth, that First Officer Wren just did," Commander Sitla replied. "Officers, do you know how stressful it is to be alone, planning and deciding what the next moves should be by oneself? Of course I was well trained and went through all the alternatives that were open to me in the absence of guidance from the leadership in Sig. In the end, it was decided that for all search spaceships like ours, designed with one mission alone, the commander in charge would have total freedom to bring the journey to an end when he or she deemed it fit to do so. If that included destroying the crew and the ships far away from Sig planet, no aspersions would ever be laid at their memory or at them personally for their decision to do what they deemed was necessary to do."

"We understand that undertaking as well, Commander Sitla," said Elle, of social engineering. "Like you, Sir, we were also taught well on what our duties were, and chief amongst them was to maintain discipline and loyalty to our commanding officer. We were told that we were to follow his directive without question, whatever our commander decided to do. As we were chosen to be a part of the planning committee, we should consider ourselves fortunate. Even if what was asked by our commander was barbarous in any way, we were to give the benefit of the doubt to our commander's decision. Do you see our dilemma, Commander?"

"I can indeed, and I understand it perfectly, Officer Elle. Indeed, I appreciate all that you have expounded so graphically. Equally, hearing from our expert ethicist, I ask, do you see any problem with implanting a deity into such a neo-population?"

Elle enquired, "Why do you feel it necessary to introduce the concept of a deity, Commander?"

Karl interrupted: "Sir, we have travelled across an almost biological empty cosmos to date until now. Most of the way, when there was any unusual phenomenon, we stopped, studied the phenomenon and tested our hypotheses, and everything was documented and sent off to Sig. This was done in the hope of adding new knowledge to our civilization. You allowed us freedom to discuss our understandings and interpretations and to log them without due diligence. Was it so because you trusted our professional knowledge? There is no right or wrong way to carry out this mission because there are enough inbuilt barriers to unethical behaviour within the ship and its crew.

"My question is, why do we need a deity or a god? We had none while we were travelling, and neither did we have a need for any on planet Sig. I knew that there were mysticisms, but none involved a deity or any god that interceded for any reason."

## More Than Just a Commander

Commander Sitla stood up, and for the first time the staff saw him smile briefly. "Of course you are correct given the way we were taught on Sig. In fact, we do not have an understanding of what a deity is, although we do understand the concept intellectually and more so philosophically.

"As to how it works and what was or is its benefit, this must be left as a theoretical debate at schools of higher learning and left within the humanities discipline."

He looked up at the ceiling of the large conference room and then muttered loudly as if to himself, but his audience listened, "Thirty billion light years ago we, the race of Sig, calculated that the universe began after a tremendous power surge. From that power awakening, all the planets and stars were formed. With all that power, extreme heat, explosive gasses, massive amounts of amalgam and alloy combinations of elements have been present in that rich inorganic soup of unknown elements."

He paused for a moment before continuing. "From inorganic to organic, under massive heat and with light-related forces of power, simple basic biological nucleic acids were also formed. By chance, these combined to form a complex that allowed beings such a microbes to be formed and distributed throughout the cosmos.

"Again by chance, these microbes entered primitive aquatic plant life and did what they do naturally: they broke down substrates using knowledge in its simple recorded incidence on how to use enzymes to do this task. The basic biological cell grew larger as it easily absorbed nutrients as a result. They then multiplied. Are you all following me? Yes, of course, all basic knowledge you were fed to believe and never questioned."

He paused again, then quietly spoke, "About twenty-eight billion years later, our scientists predicted that the basics required for biological life had begun. This theory was open to conjecture in my day and could be justified to some extent by what our predecessors experienced and what we as a race of explorers have experienced as we travelled across the cosmos."

In the silence that followed, the conference room became lighted as the ship completed another orbit around the sun. This space vessel was the height of magnificence in technological engineering, created by the scientists of Sig. The crew sat in silence as the old commander got up and walked around the room.

Looking up suddenly, he said, "I put to you the fact that many molecules came together to form metals and biochemical products. And the first link of genetic acid bases may not have been an accident or coincidence but rather the product of a thoughtful creative design."

Anne was the first to speak up: "From a philosophical standpoint, that would be the premise for a distinct scholarly discussion. But we have scientific evidence of our own evolution from a single cell to us, a complex biological entity. We have in our genetic design that phenotypical manifestation of us as biological beings. We originated from the ability of our thinking minds that developed by overcoming obstacles." She paused.

She continued once her mind had placed her arguments into logical order. "What were the roots and reasons for the biological species of Sig to become an advanced entity among the stars of the cosmos? Was it not through our own ingenuity? It was the ability of abstract thought and science, which we have mastered. We are a benign race that has looked after our own development and has not taken part in any form of savagery. We look after the welfare of our species, and that is what we are trying to spread to similar biological primate species. Is that not our mandate, Commander?"

Commander Sitla replied, "Anne, you are jumping ahead of time. There was a why before all that came to pass. Can you get your mind around that fact? Why was our planet a veritable garden that had all the necessities for our survival and development? Why were there no scourges of diseases as seen here, no aggressive behaviour between us and the animal species that live in our forests and savannahs? Why was there just enough water and sunshine from to nurture biological life forms, and why we are allowed to live so long?

"Why were there no massive meteors or cosmic catastrophes on Sig as we see evidence of on almost all the planets we have seen and visited on our way here? I put it all to you to think whether we were created for a reason, and if so, what was that reason, and who or what was the reasoner?"

# SECTION III

A Scholar Earthling of the Future Interprets

# CHAPTER 8

# Deity—a Necessity for Humanoids

Author Les muttered to himself, "This is an even stranger piece of Sanskrit." He looked at it curiously. "Will you have a look at this cuneiform lettering?" the old man asked Alice, his researcher wife. She was already looking up similar ancient Arabic hieroglyphs, making notes and references. She stopped, went over to her husband and took the block away. "Leave it with me. I think I might have seen this type of scribbling before. I will chase up my notes. You carry on," she coaxed him.

While Alice never said anything to Les about it, she rather enjoyed these literature searches because she learnt much from reading scientific journals similar to reading a novel or textbook. She took her time when researching the different aspects required for each item Les was working on. To support his findings or to remove doubt, she did the research. She was quite thorough in searching the literature even when he was not specific in what he asked her to chase up from the archives of ancient literature.

As a result, Alice downloaded an eclectic mixture of information from the world libraries that included English translations as found in the Library of Congress in New York.

Her little problem was in fact a distraction in that she was easily led onto a path she found interesting but that had nothing to do with their research. After a time, when he asked of her progress and did not get a response, he assumed that she was focused elsewhere.

However, unlike his younger self, he would stop what he was doing and join her in the interests she had uncovered, even when it had absolutely nothing to do with their project. This would put their research on hold as their discussions led into different tangents and outlooks. "What great companionship," he said while they were having tea.

As a result, the planned day's work would not be completed. Les would call for a pause and time out, usually with the suggestion, "How about a glass of wine, some cold Italian meats, cheddar, a crusty baguette and olives?"

"Wonderful" would be the bouncy reply.

The bent figure went to his desk and fingered the black cubes that were left on his wife's desk. He placed them back into the box and kept all in order, pending their return to the project. Before leaving his desk, he would continue writing on his computer, his concentration mesmerized with the activity, until he was called several times: "Come on, lunch is ready [or it's snack time]; come and get it."

Strange thoughts passed through the old man's mind as he sipped his coffee in the darkness of a January winter's morning. He looked at his day planner and found he was a full day behind, but strangely this did not have the seething impact on his mind and attitude as it would have done when he was in his sixties or even into his seventies. There was a strange calmness that had come over him on this project.

As a prolific dreamer, Les invariably had two other manuscripts on the go in his old computer. He could quite easily get into a manuscript and lose himself for hours or work until his eyes got tired. When this happened, he would nod off for a while, only to awaken and continue as if nothing had happened where he had left off on the manuscript.

*No!* he thought to himself. He was rather enjoying this search because he did not have any deadline to meet as in his younger college days. He loved using old Churchillian language and the language of George Bernard Shaw, Oscar Wilde and the critics of the day. Later on, he embellished his conversations with quotations from Greek and Latin tales as anecdotes. Probably the best thing about entertaining his retired friends over their early breakfasts and supper gatherings was his ability to quote a piece of poetry that would be unacceptable in today's society of political correctness.

"Ah! I have been blessed to live long and to witness wonderful changes in society." The old author's mind was in conflict with regard to what he had learned about being scholarly as a boy and the use of the English language by the parliamentarians of the 1950s. He revelled in his scholarly upbringing, which might have been the reason for his gentle demeanour. However, using such language among today's group of youths would reveal the arrogance of an age past, one that no longer existed. "However," he mumbled, "so much of it has remained with me over my eight decades plus."

He continued speaking to himself: "This introspection cannot be healthy. Yes, yes, I know the trouble is that the new generation will not understand what I have written. The old days of satire and irony in scholarly conversation, as in the days of Oscar Wilde and George Bernard Shaw, have been lost to the modern-day student. Only those few who still go to the performing arts theatres to enjoy an evening with a period play such as one written by Shakespeare or Shaw would know what it was like."

Interrupting himself, he said, "Well, I had better get on interpreting this cube; all this romanticism will not get me any further in its translation." He began to scan the new pile of documents that his wife had printed out and left on top of his computer.

"Religion is important to the whole existence of humankind. It played an essential role in evolution, says one religious anthropologist." He spoke to himself, "This should spell out a different perspective.

"In the evolutionary development of a primate with a functioning brain and living under the terrors of the environment, it was necessary for said primate to protect itself continually from storms and attacks by wild animals and fellow hominids. It was sensible to retreat into caves, away from these terrors."

Mumbling to himself, he continued, "While hunting or stalking in itself was a blood-related necessity, at short notice one would have to retreat for protection, running into an unknown cave that may have been the home of a sabre-toothed tiger lurking in the darkness, or a female mountain lion, or a wild black bear looking after her cubs, all of which could be quite disconcerting.

"Caves were the homes of many living animals, from biting poisonous spiders, snakes and scorpions to large animals. This would have instilled a built-up level of stress, causing early humankind always to be on the alert. Could living under such extenuating conditions be the reason that a hominid would develop an aggressive attitude? If this was a defence strategy for survival, it could possibly develop into a trait that would be passed down to subsequent generations.

"Consequently, living with a continual phase of aggressive behaviour might have contributed to the trait of bloodthirstiness as an essential part of survival. However, could this have led to brain development?"

The old author put down the papers, sipped his now cold coffee and looked up at the dreary daylight outside his window. The house was quiet because his wife slept in every morning. This gave his mind time to think and surmise situations in isolation. "Oh, what peace there is in silence!" He yawned.

To himself his thoughts ran: *I wonder if the implication is that the darkness of sinful aggressive behaviour is an essential part of humankind's or Homo sapiens' survival mechanism?* His mind continued: *Then is it possible that this inscription explains the savagery of humankind as a natural part of our humanity? That would not be a bad thing if one was to place education as a result of practical living into the mix. It could partially explain the case of using that aggressive trait to focus on moving ahead against all obstacles and being persistent. It must be why humankind has been successful as the dominant primate on this planet.*

Out loud he said, "My assumption: the makeup of humankind is like two sides of the same coin. On the one side is latent savagery developed from an aggressive trait, and on the other side is the gentler, peace-loving human that has an evolved a psyche of kindness towards his fellow man. Educated humankind is evolving into a gentler race; however, some humans may lack this brain development and conceivably are able to kill with no regret or emotion.

"This aggressive behaviour has become an essential trait in the criminal mind. Even if it is only partial, human beings could use their gift of choice and follow an aggressive nature because it may have morphed into an addiction. But will there still be the good trait within the individual if it remains suppressed, and if so, why?"

Savagery, an essential trait in the evolution of humankind. The old man, searching for answers to the puzzle of ancient artifacts, thought aloud:

"The writing is quite clear: God is real inside humanity, and the conflict between doing good or doing evil is essential to our survival. Free will allows humankind to choose which path to take. History has shown hordes of men streaming along on horseback or in bands, killing and raping in their fight to take over territories. In more modern times, under a more civil society, this trait of savagery is being used to protect injustices committed by one group upon another. However, the slaughter of large numbers of humans remains an enigma to the educated mind as it is still practised today.

"A so-called 'developed' society of people accept their modern army's killing of citizens of another country from a distance with the intent of exploiting the economy of the enemy. How does the civilized mind cope with seeing the detriment of others who suffer as a result? The world wars under Nazism, the Golden Horde of Genghis Khan, the Romans in their need to conquer more territory, used organized, well-trained armies under intelligent ruthless leaders wanting to rule the world at that time.

"A young Alexander the Great, at the age of seventeen years, rode with his band of Macedonians and conquered the old enemies of his country, after which he took over their lands and cities. One can understand such an action when one's country is exploited by a stronger army. He wanted to be free of intimidation by another race, and he set out to take back all that had been taken away from his people. However, seething within his breast was the beast that wanted revenge for the past. He killed the enemies whom he felt were a threat to him and his people."

Les the aged author continued to think. "As his conquests continued, he left behind an organized team of administrators to run the captured cities and countries by extracting taxes, which were sent back to Macedonia and the Greek empire.

"Alexander's addiction to power and the use of might, essentially his bloodthirstiness, had become dominant in his makeup when he was a youth. He was a youth who knew no fear, and his imagination knew no limit. Driven by youthful internal strength, he moved from country to country and made Macedonia leader in his world for the time being. He saw no bounds to his strength and his imagination."

*What is the deduction from this vague hypothesis?* asked the old author of his mind. *Is it then that evil is an essential trait in the makeup of humankind just as goodness is? And they share a part of the spirit or soul equally in each human on planet Earth?*

*Does it follow that humankind chooses to be either the devil or the saint? But what allows a person to make one choice over another? After all, human beings have free will, and we developed into a civilized society. If that is so, is this the god within each human that humankind seeks out in the heavens? How does this equate with the greater power of the universe and the fact that it suddenly erupted from a big bang of powerful energy?*

Another sip of the cold coffee took the old man to his comfortable chair. He had been standing while reading the reprints that his wife had left on his desk before she went to bed.

Muttering to himself, Les said, "I believe that inherently humankind looks towards the heavens searching for our Deity and God because that is where our immortal spirit or soul originated, a location that neither time nor space can explain because of our earthly limitations, but it is from whence all souls are derived. Science finds this concept unfounded, especially when dealing with evolutionary philosophy. In earthly terms, a person with some religious exposure can accept that part of the human psyche and realize it as a component known to the soul."

Unseen, a shadow slid across the room. The old man glanced towards the ceiling and dismissed the shadow as maybe a blink of electricity.

"Mmm! I am looking for that single grain of sand on a beach." The old man continued with his thought process as his developed brain quietly scanned his cerebral files. These mental files had developed over the years from experiences and learned studies of ancient scripts. Added to his imagination and the hard sciences, his was a knowledge of one concoction. From this wealth of knowledge he was trying to decipher or sift out one piece of the puzzle.

"Of course, in many ancient religious beliefs, human souls are spiritual energy derived from the cosmos and therefore are indestructible or immortal from a religious philosophical perspective. The cosmos is the source of different types of energies that humankind will never be able to fathom in one lifetime or in future generations of the species.

"On the other hand, evolved humankind only searches for the energy that is measured through our created laws of physics and chemistry. Such an approach is shallow and limited when considered amidst the profound concept of what reality is in the cosmos. Deep within humankind, the spirit or soul seeks the source from whence we were created."

# CHAPTER 9

# Cube No. 1: Death and the Afterlife

আমরা দেবতা সুপ্রিম এর স্বর্গীয় মহিমা
উপর ধ্যান
পৃথিবীর অন্তরে কে আছে
আকাশের জীবন এবং স্বর্গের আত্মার
ভিতরে
তিনি আমাদের মনকে উদ্দীপিত করেন
এবং আলোকিত করেন

Cube No. 1

Translation:
We meditate on the transcendental
Glory of the Deity Supreme
Who is inside the heart of the earth,
Inside the life of the sky and inside the
Soul of heaven.
May he stimulate and
Illuminate our minds.

> Om bhur bhuvah svah
> Tat savitur varenyam
> Bhargo devasya dhimahl
> Dhiyo yonah prachodayat.

*In the Hindu philosophy it is believed that at death, all souls return to the Source or their origin before entering a second reincarnation as an earthling or some other living species in the universe. Does that mean that all life forms have evolved from the cosmos, including the botanical species? Yes is the answer. Since humankind has no definition of what a soul is, we do not look at other bioforms as having souls.* So went the thinking of Les.

*They are living; therefore, they may have a questionable form or an abstract intangible state. In humans it is called "feeling" and "emotion," but for other life forms, such a phenomenon is unknown at this stage, or so I believe.*

Speaking aloud to himself in his office, Les went on: "If I continue with this type of diatribe, I shall be put away very quickly and indefinitely."

Again a shadow passed over the room.

## The Wisdom of a Young Child

Looking at the blank screen of his computer, Les paused and thought, *What was it my young grandson, at the age of six, said to* me? Mmm, "You cannot choose what you want to be when you return, Granddad."

Yes, I remember our little chat when I said, to tease him, "Well, my little man, I have only had my seventy-ninth birthday. I would like to come back as an eagle and soar through the skies."

Grandson was quite firm: "Sorry, Granddad, you cannot choose what you wish to be when you return after death."

My response: "Well, why not?"

He replied, "You will come back as a living being."

"Do you mean like a tree, or like a worm that a robin could peck at and digest?"

"I do not know about a worm, but maybe a tree would be OK."

I replied, "Then I would like to return as a redwood giant that will live for three thousand years. That would be nice."

Out of the mouths of babes. This grandson of mine quietly informed me when he was four that I did not have to worry about dying. When I asked why, he said, "You will come back like a baby." When I asked how he knew that, he said that he was with many babies. Later on, we were chatting about friends and how important they are to everyone because he had just broken up with a new friend he had met at camp.

He asked if I had any friends, and I said that I had many but that my best friend had died. He asked what my friend was called. I told him, and when I looked at him, he had a broad smile on his face. He said, "I know him. We were babies together." My friend had an unusual name, and I knew my grandson had not met anyone with such a name.

After a discussion with the rest of the family, we thought he had a "Hindu gene" because he had related reincarnation, which forms the basis of the Hindu religion.

"There are more things in heaven and earth, Horatio" came to mind because of the fact that a child of six years old had seen, in his new home, a woman standing in the corridor in a white dress. His mother asked where she was, and he pointed to the empty corridor. She saw an empty corridor, not what he saw. A few weeks later she asked if the woman was still in *the house. He quietly said, "No! She left a long time ago," and continued playing with his Lego set.*

*On another occasion he and his mother went to pick up his dad from a long-term-care hospital where he had been working. It was late evening as his dad was finishing his shift at 9:00. They parked outside on the driveway of the hospital with no other cars around. They entered the empty foyer that was well-lit, and my grandson ran off. His mother called out to him to return and not run so fast. He did not appear to hear her as he was across the room. She called to him again. He turned and came back to her, saying, "Sorry, Mum, I cannot hear you with all these people speaking so loudly. Can you not hear them?"*

*They were the only two people in the large foyer. She asked what he meant. He spoke loudly, "Hey, you ghosts, stop speaking. I cannot hear my mum." Turning to her, he said, "Look, Mum, they are all around us, so many of them, speaking very loudly."*

Les, looking through his window absent-mindedly, thought, *I do not believe in ghosts, but there does appear to be a supernatural link that children before the age of six seem to have. It has been documented as anecdotal evidence. They seem able to see the spirits of the departed, and they are not afraid of them. In the case of Grandson, he seemed to remember a great deal of experience before he was born or, as he said, from when he was a baby.*

Les knew he was mentally rambling, but this was how he began writing: "I am open to different forms of understanding, and while I do not wish to see the spirits of others as Grandson did, I do think that there might be something to this reincarnation philosophy. Do these ephemeral beings return to those they left behind? I do not believe that this is so, but they do return under different circumstances and to different families.

"This is my belief, and it has become stronger now that the impact of my ageing is palpable. Maybe it is just wishful thinking as my time gets closer, but it is comforting to know there is life after death.

"Grandson once said to me that he came back to make Grammy and me happy, as well as his mum and dad."

Les continued reminiscing aloud: "When does human imagination begin—I mean, at what age? My little man could not have imagined all that he said to us because, as with all children, he was honesty personified. So supposing he responded because his nosy granddad had asked such questions, and he felt in his little way he had to answer. Why answer with such knowledgeable insight?

"That there are mysteries in life of the spiritual world or the incarnate, there is no question. From the time of the pyramids, there has been a great infatuation with death and the afterlife, which is attributed to the building of great tombs filled with the material goods of this world. It is a simplistic interpretation of what life after death might really be. In fact, an individual's mortality is the final act on this earth while still in this earthly physical form that one is endowed with, so it appears to make sense."

Les's wife, Alice, entered the office with two cups of tea in hand: "You are up a bit early. What are you up to?" she asked.

"Ah! Morning, my pretty one," he happily replied as all his current thoughts disappeared from his mind. But he continued, "The usual stuff. Why are we here? Who made helium and that sort of stuff, you know." The old couple broke up laughing.

Alice asked, "Does that mean you would like to have cooked oatmeal this morning?"

Les replied, "How did you guess? And it would be ever so nice if there was a bit of honey and some cinnamon powder sprinkled over the top. Mmm!"

They sat quietly and sipped their tea. Since the old man now had company, he spoke up, "You know, old thing, this block or cube has given me a hypothesis that might make a good spot in a novel. Suppose that the earth, the trees and all life forms on this planet, including us, are all inextricably tied together as long as we live. Even after death, there would remain an immortal part of us that cannot be divested from the planet."

Alice said, "Now that you have put it in that light, it is not a bad idea. When one thinks that all living things on this planet have evolved together and the planet is still an active and living thing, there is merit to such a theory. It therefore stands to reason there might be codependency that is intangible to us masses of living beings. But if all life forms are part of the heritage of life specific to Earth, and given that Earth is a living planet, theoretically if one part leaves, then the integrity of all life would be under threat. Life would not be the same if one piece were to disappear completely. If, however, a life changes from one form to another, then the sum of life remains the same on the planet. Yes, we might be inextricably tied to our planet where we have all evolved."

Les, smiling, said, "Aha! Matter is neither created nor destroyed— the first article in science. You know, I am going to fly with that concept."

# CHAPTER 10

# Uncharted Territory

Les, the enquiring scientist, said, "The greyish-white thread-like inscription appears to be from either the Mayan encrypted alphabet or from ancient Greek translation. Looks like confusion again, for these Cyrillic drawings or writings leave me cold. I just do not have the education, but worst of all, I have no interest in this subject. Now let us see what my clever spouse has interpreted. It is the word *pleroma*. Reading Genesis from the Greek Orthodox interpretation, I see that the translation means 'the happiness or pain designated by a living structure of the fullness of things.'

"That does not sound too ominous, but why such a dictate, and what is the purpose of this inscription? One wonders if these blocks were written as a guide for human society. If these blocks are of alien origin and were meant for the evolving human race to find, why was this necessary? Who was it that had our best interests at heart? Who on earth at that time had the skills and knowledge?"

Les continued: "Block number six describes a religious state where humans believed, as laid out in the book of Genesis in the Old Testament, that God created humankind, the earth and all the animals and plants. Humankind lived, according to Genesis of the Old Testament, in the garden of perfection called Eden. This garden housed all the wondrous things the new humans Adam and Eve could ever have desired. But were these new creations loyal to their Creator, who had provided all that humankind could ever desire?"

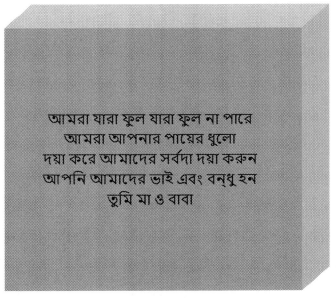

Block No. 6

Jo khila sake na vo phaala ham hai.
Tumhaare charanon ki dhoola ham hai.
Dayaa kee drishti sadaa hi rakhanaa.
Tumhi ho bandhu sakhaa tumhi ho.

We are those flowers that could not blossom.
We are the dust of your feet.
Please, always have compassion on us.

You are our brother and friend.
You are Mother and Father.

Hindi:
हम उन फूल हैं जो खिल नहीं सकते
हम आपके पैरों की धूल हैं
कृपया हमेशा हमारे साथ दया करें
आप हमारे भाई और दोस्त हैं
आप माँ और पिता हैं

Les had read Catholic and Presbyterian passages in his lifetime. The Bible stories were ingrained in him as a boy. The Bible had great adventures that depicted hate, love, lust and murder. *All of which makes for good novel writing,* he thought to himself.

*Humans were given free will, which implies independence from everyone, including God. However, these first two beings were happy and told God they were. So a little test was given to measure humankind's obedience to the laws as laid down by their Creator. There is confusion in the logic here as to why a Creator who made humankind in his own perfect image would wish to quality-control himself by posing a challenge. The Creator was perfect, and he was the only model around from which he copied himself. Now he wished to see if he'd done a good job?*

*Ahem! Am I missing a piece of logic here?* Les thought.

*That the Creator made the perfect being to fit his perfect image in a perfect garden is a given. After all, the Creator is perfection and purity and all that these traits imply. However, in a generous decision, he broke down in order to give his creation sway over their future in the form of free will. It happened that they used the gift of free will to do something they were asked not to do. From here on philosophical discussions in the modern age gave no answers as to why punishment was necessary.*

Les started in on an aside, following his author's wandering mind, this time speaking aloud: "In today's technical world, powerful news media appear to demand that all information be transparent and the public be given the freedom to interpret the news. Hence, using their unlimited resources, these pundits of the media have uncovered that there is a belief/philosophy that postures that God resides in every living being, including both botanical and zoological life forms in nature.

"Their documentary findings show that humankind has a choice and can choose to do 'bad' things as well as 'good' things. In the formation days, 'God,' the voice within, asked human beings not to eat of the fruit from one tree. By God's allowing a sinful voice to flatter these newborn humans, saying it was the 'fruit of knowledge,' humankind did not think twice and ate from the tree. Humankind failed the one challenge posed by their Creator by using their free will. It was here that humankind found knowledge of what was right and what was wrong. They chose." Absent-mindedly, Les squeezed the cube in his hand.

Again a shadow crossed the room. Mumbling to himself, Les said, "I should check the electrical system.

"Humankind's punishment was to be left alone in their nakedness to find their way and to experience pain and happiness of their making. They had to experience all that was good and bad from their surroundings, but while it was paradise, they experienced all that was good. Where would they find 'bad' experiences or knowledge of what bad was? Or was it just disobedience for which they were punished? After Adam's disobedience, he began to grow and evolve. Using his cosmic freedom to achieve knowledge through experimentation of both 'good' and 'bad,' his evolution began. It was not really a scolding but rather an opportunity to educate himself."

The old writer continued to think out loud: "Why was there a need for humankind to have a power greater than themselves? The biblical reference stipulates humankind was given power over all that was in their environment. The other question that puzzles is, why does humankind look upwards into the sky to pray and to seek answers from that greatest of all powers? Is it that in doing so, we witness the beauty and power of the universe? It lies there empty except for the stars, laid out in a pattern for us to one day explore, gaining knowledge and using its resources."

With a future portend, Les declared, "So humankind will eventually find our way there in the universe, but it will not be easy. In fact, our greatest enlightenment will happen because we will have to fight our way through tremendous cosmic obstacles. Only by overcoming these will humankind learn to survive in the cosmos from whence our immortal souls originated.

"It is strange that in many religious philosophies there exists the same expression of having a mother, a father and brothers in heaven— that they are all one and thus can help when there is a need. The problem with asking for celestial assistance is that one would never learn if one had help. It is known now that one learns from one's experience and mainly from one's mistakes. So what does humankind need from a celestial God? Is it sympathy? Is it for a miracle to raise a relative from death? One of the main lessons on leaving Eden was that humankind would face death similar to the cycle of life that animals and plants undergo."

*Cycle of life, the same for humankind,* Les thought to himself. "Plants return when their seeds germinate, and animals after fertilization of an ovum that brings forth a new life after pregnancy. So how does a single human being return? One solution hypothesized is that when the body is destroyed, falling into dust or ashes, the soul returns to the creative force of the cosmos. Speculation would suggest that after a time, the soul will return as a new baby. Oh heck! That is old Hindu reincarnation teachings!"

A shadow crossed the room. Les casually looked upwards.

# CHAPTER 11

# Religious Dogma: Greek Orthodox Interpretation of Genesis

The Greek Orthodox patristic teachings never hesitate to tackle scientific dogma, not even after hypothesis extends and testing proves to be either true or false. Patristic beliefs or faith goes on to prove its point because science does not believe in faith. It uses hypotheses and theories and makes its own rules that eventually prove to be a truth or a falsehood within a limited framework.

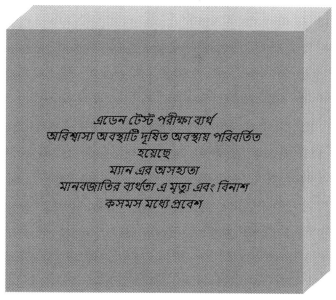

Block No. 4

Failing the Test in Eden

The
Incorrupt status changed to a corrupted state.
The futility of humankind.
Death and destruction entered the cosmos at the
Failure of humankind.

From
The Orthodox patristic belief in
Anthropology, soteriology
And eschatology.[1]

---

[1] Soteriology: teaching espousing the original incorruption of humankind's immortal soul, an immortal gift from God. Soteriology is connected to eschatology.

Hindi:
ईडन में परीक्षा नाकाम रही
अस्थिर स्थिति को भ्रष्ट स्थिति में बदल दिया गया
मनुष्य की निरर्थकता
मौत और विनाश मानव जाति की विफलता में ब्रह्मांड में प्रवेश किया

In the small office, Les again noticed that the lights appeared to be dim. In an authorial mood, Les was reading his notes:

> Humankind is a savage with the potential for unlimited cruelty, manifesting a beastly behaviour towards its own kind. As a result, human beings exercise their physical strength through brutality in order to dominate a foe, a family, and later on countries and other races, overtly attacking their brothers and sisters.

> Humankind began as a simple dictator, and in today's society, as seen in Africa, heads of tribes of one kind begin attacking another. What is the reason? Is it to gain domination over resources as seen in Nigeria and Somalia? That is one acceptable explanation interpreted by the rest of the watching world.

He read to himself: "Should one consider that the souls of such men had become corrupted to the extent that physical, hurtful power dominated their being? The majority of these despots did not get satisfactory pleasure from their conquests. Real pleasure does not belong to the flesh but to the actions of the soul, which at birth is uncorrupted. Human pleasure became diseased, and that led to the law of the savage. It is losing the supernatural quality of one's soul, a created phenomenon, and that is a meaningful destruction."

Classic example: a shadow again floated across the room when

Les touched the onyx cube. With his aged eyesight, he just blamed the fleeting shadows to floaters and to his geriatric state.

He continued reading his notes: "Greed had become the motive of Mayan leaders that drove them to conquer and to accumulate a greater share of earth's wealth for personal selfish reasons. They did this by attacking and killing the surrounding tribes, but it was mainly the leaders who went to war, not the workers who produced the food.

"After a time, the leaders or elders in the Mayan hierarchy lost the ability to lead. There was no pleasure even though they had the power of many workers. They became addicted to causing pain and indulged in sacrificial killing to appease the God of the universe. Soon physical pain became a sensible pleasure, and their leadership became skewed in their minds.

"As a result, workers were not told when to plant or when to reap the crops. Once the crops of beans and corn were used up and no replanting had taken place, the tribes began to starve. They could not make a living from the forests, so the workers scattered in the absence of leadership."

Les felt the author inside burning within him: "Ah! The power of greed. Let me see: the tribes in South America almost disappeared completely thorough senseless wars. However, the societies left behind pyramids that deteriorated into cracked stone structures, and traces of advanced buildings were slowly overgrown by the surrounding forests."

## Anthropological Evolution

*Environmental Greed*

"Through the millennia, humankind took with impunity all they wanted from the botanical and marine world. With thoughtless indiscrimination, humankind withdrew too much, too quickly, leaving a huge challenge for these life forms to recover within the vast forests and aquatic accumulations on the planet. The Creator made all life forms on this planet, and to date Earth is the only planet that has evolved to be an example of all that is possible. Human beings, in the early days, never replaced or nurtured the biological life forms on which they depended for food, heat and comfort."

## Les's Observation

"It was not possible for the environment to be sustained with continual rapid depletion. Today large areas of the planet are reverting to become deserts, while the oceans are becoming lifeless through overexploitation of their life forms.

"Without our understanding the dynamic intertwining of all life forms on the planet, many species have gone extinct because of the main predator's actions on planet Earth. On the other hand, at Adam's birth, it was heard that God had given him permission: 'I give you dominion over the birds in the air, the fish in the oceans and all the animals and plants in the forests.'

"That was taken literally by the preachers of religion, but there were fewer humans on the planet at the time. With the increased human population, more was taken out from the bounteous earth's ecosystem than could be renewed in time."

The author mumbled to himself while reading the reprinted pages left by his still-asleep spouse.

"However, a male leader evolved from the early family phase to be the hunter and provider for the family. In return he extracted a 'payment' in the form of comfort from the physically weaker humanoids surrounding him."

Les the author said, "Yes! Yes! In particular from the female of the species, who provided physical comfort to her savage companion in the form of warmth on cold days and who satisfied the physical need for copulation.

"Ah! Primitive man had a need for codependency in his cave, and if an offspring came from his female, it meant little to him at the time."

Les continued mumbling under his breath: "Later on, this

offspring, who was protected by the powerful and strong instinct within the female, had value. Holding off the comfort of 'human' companionship by the female against the male to protect her young, the offspring had clout. The simpler male knew that this was a trade-off. He became head of the family, sharing the food brought back from his labour in the field. This pleased the female as she had control of the food, and that directly influenced the nutrition of the offspring. The hunter's reward was food prepared accompanied by a promise of warmth and sex.

"Eventually the value of an offspring, if male, added to the ageing hunter's comfort now that he was becoming unable to be the main provider. The male offspring would have learnt hunting from his father through observation on a hunt. He followed what had become practice and began to share his successfully hunted game, the food resource, with the family. Protection of this family unit rested with the physical power that was now in possession of the younger, stronger males.

"The females gathered food found in the forests, such as nuts, roots and vegetation, and added them to the diet, thus increasing health. A female offspring had a different value, as a commodity to be used, as barter for another male desiring a partner, thus increasing the old male's possession and wealth. However, such a daughter/spouse, after comforting the young hunter, would insist that her ageing family also share in his successful hunt."

## God's Latent Message

The author, thinking aloud, said, "I wonder if we have not missed another value of an offspring. Look at our own grandson at age three or four. I was physically unable to bend down and do physical things on the floor as more supple granddads can do with their grandchildren. He came along when we were much older. We had the joy of being with a young, trusting little man who brought out deep love from us old grandparents."

Les smiled gently, thinking of the past, so many years ago, when one daughter gave them a beautiful grandson.

"Yes, we were very happy. I remember how our grandson said to us that he came to make us happy, and he did indeed," Les reminisced.

Les, always looking for the seeds of conversations to be used when he was the author, recaptured the conversation: "Grammy told him to have a chat with Granddad in the sunroom as she prepared the evening meal.

She said, 'Archer, your granddad is in the sunroom reading a treatise on a possible candidate for sainthood within the Greek Orthodox Church.'

Here is what Granddad had learnt from this grandson at age three. His little man moved from the love seat to the couch as any restless youthful child would do.

On this occasion he asked, 'Granddad, are you old?'

My reply: 'Of course, Grandson, I am old. You were just a little baby in my arms three years ago. Now you are three years old. All living things get old. Why do you ask?'

He retorted, 'Well, you will get older then.' He paused and twisted his neck at a slant.

"'What does that mean?' I asked.

He quietly replied, 'You will die.'

I smiled and said, 'Of course, one day I will die.'

He looked at me with puzzled eyes, unemotional. 'I do not want you and Grammy to die!'

I looked at pure innocence personified and quietly replied, 'Well, Grandson, we do not intend to die as yet. We want to live and see you grow up, so do not worry.'

Moving from chair to couch, he replied, 'Well, you do not have to worry, you know, because Mother Nature will bring you back as a baby. You can begin all over again.'

"Geriatric dementia," the old author spoke to himself. His soliloquy: "On the other hand, the spirit went off to the core of the universe from whence it originated. It would return. So it is with all the babies that are born. No one pays attention to these little angels given to us by a benign Creator. We continue to nurture them, but we do not ask them, when they are only three or four years old, all the things we always wanted to know. By the age of six, Archer no longer said anything to us, and when we asked about what he had told us, he had forgotten."

The author, looking up at the ceiling of his office, spoke quietly: "I believe, and I do not wish anyone to try to change my old mind. I give thanks to my wonderful parents, who brought us up as Christians. Just as the Saviour returned from death to report to us, I know there is reincarnation. Thanks to my grandson, he verified all that I ever wanted to know. I love that little man, now grown up and in university."

# CHAPTER 12

# Cosmic Plans for the Future

"As first officer, I can inform this planning group of the anthropologists' report, but we have already discussed most of what is in it. In short, I propose that as a project management task we take a few thousand circles around their sun as a time measurement for this planet. In this way we might be able to measure the success of our superficial initiatives in guiding this population of primates. We should place ourselves into a slowed metabolism but set the alarm for our recovery at one thousand of their orbital periods of three hundred and sixty-five days.

"Keep the files open on the data we have worked on today. On awakening, we will let the computers bring us up to date. This is the only way, if it is indeed our intention to do so, to make this planet habitable and place it on the course to becoming a worthwhile civilized world. However, whenever a piece of intellectual abstraction is made or wisdom is abstracted, let there be an unobtrusive recorder to note their awakening intelligence from the cues we will have left them."

He continued, "Of course this work will be our lifelong engagement until we ourselves die off. Once every member of the crew knows of our purpose, our actions will be justified. It is up to our ethics experts to render justification for this undertaking. Since we will not all die at the same time, every one of us must work to nudge the different races and tribes in the various geographic locations forward. It is necessary at this stage that they should all be progressing at similar rates. Such a plan should provide enough incentive to leave vigorous and ambitious civilizations of humanoids on this beautiful blue planet."

Looking at all the keen managers of the different plans, he summed up: "Re-evaluating our work and making adjustments to the project plans, we may be able to judge their future as a civilization." He paused as all eyes focused on him.

He looked tired but raised his resolute face towards them. "We will not be around to see their growth and development or to observe when they will one day travel the universe. We hope that when they do, they will find planet Sig's location. That should end our civilization's loneliness."

Commander Sitla spoke up: "I have no opposition to this lengthy plan. If we sow the correct seeds, the cosmos will reveal their future challenge, as it has done for us. Should one race get ahead of the other tribes, they should initiate the effort to pool their knowledge, physical resources and human power to get into space. On the other hand, competition between the tribes or races would allow for speed in innovation. After this, they will form associations that will promulgate advancement towards such a grand goal. Surely that will fire their collective imagination."

"Tread carefully, my commander," responded Elle, the social engineer, who until now had remained quiet. She continued, "Do not be so quick to promote this idea. We are looking at a primitive evolving primate species. They possess an aggressive gene and are known to kill and to destroy other life forms as they do their own. From a social science perspective, we will inadvertently be supporting barbarism in allowing marauding bands of tribes using physical power to kill and to get what they want, not necessarily what they need."

Elle took a deep breath then continued, "Should this analogy be taken further and a member of our crew lives longer than the leading group, will it not make it easy for this person to impart knowledge under this guideline you will have left behind?"

She was becoming enthusiastic for what she had in mind. "We may have to impart knowledge for building weapons to industrial proportions for power-seeking individuals and organizations. The worst outlook would be that one day, such groups could use very advanced weaponry made for armies to employ against their own kind. How will this end up? Maybe using military engineering power to destroy their own kind in mass battles taking place from distant continents? Will this end justify the possibility that we may be guiding these tribes to attack each other in the hope of modeling a subgroup that may one day return to planet Sig?"

She paused, looked down at her feet, then continued: "My fear goes deeper. What exactly would such a population with power wish to do if or when they entered space? Would they really wish to join Sig's benign population, which will appear as weak and defenceless? Who is to know what such an enhanced evolved race of hominids released into the great cosmos would want to do? Would they, in fact, really wish to join with any other alien life forms in friendship or just use their power to dominate by attacking, in our case, our forebears?"

"You put forward a very powerful reason for not proceeding with this course of action, team member Elle," responded the Commander. "I trust that this is not the end point of your discourse, is it?" he asked.

She replied, "Of course not, Commander Sitla, but we appear to be rushing towards a conclusion and formation of the end product in our project planning without doing due diligence on possible long-term ramifications.

"What are the opinions of other teammates? What have you got to say, Anne? You were the finest geneticist to come out of our planet's academic training institute."

Anne stood up. Ignoring the comment that was meant to flatter her, she strode around the conference room of the vast ship as she would have done in one of the academic institutions on planet Sig. Academically, she had done extremely well in her studies. She would have ended up lecturing on academic probabilities without any practical experience.

She had wanted to join this crew, and to date she had wonderful practical experiences since being on board. She had aged little over her time on the ship, but the Commander's plan had caught her imagination. Now she was placed into the limelight with a questionable disagreement by the ethics expert. She walked around the table a second time. She did this to give herself time to put things in a logical order before she spoke.

"To use genetic technology to enhance a species on which we rely, such as enhancing a particular food product like a seed with a higher protein content for us to eat, is a wonderful example of genetic involvement and enhancement."

She paused. It was quite a lengthy silence. All eyes focused on her. Then she continued, "You see, this is not new to us. We all know that genetic enhancements gave the society of Sig its advanced edge that has led towards a utopic society. While it is true that the plains of Sig had a variety of tribes, we all understood each other and knew that apart from the colouring of our skin and the size of our heads, we were all the same. In comparison, and from my limited knowledge and research of this planet's hominid species, we are eight feet tall. The greatest height this species will ever attain will be about six feet, give or take a few inches, at this phase of their diet."

She again paused. "We do know the effects that our appearance has on their psyche. Remember, our heads are twice as large as theirs, in fact almost three times as large. These dimensions are not new to you or us, but how do they see us? When they saw us for the first time, they simply ran away."

The geneticist looked around at the heads of her shipmates. "You see, our eyes are larger than their fists, and much of that is due to the length of time we have spent in space in an atmosphere of low gravity." Anne stopped.

Anne did not sit down but now spoke up louder, becoming animated. "Crew mates, do you remember our stories as children in the land of make-believe? The characters described to us were either too small like midgets or too large like giants, and many had five or six digits. Some did not have arms like us but tentacles. Our imagination took over, and we felt either mirth or fear of these characters. The question I pose to you is, how do you think these primitive hominids will remember and dream of us?

"These hominids are like children with an undeveloped brain and little knowledge of technology. In this state, they are mentally vulnerable and gullible to our actions regardless of our good intentions." Her voice lowered as she continued, "You see, they may think of us as giants and demons who have invaded their territories. I dare say they will continue to make drawings of us in their caves and also make sculptures in stone and carvings on rock faces. As both previous speakers have given or suggested plans or actions to be undertaken, I would like to present from my professional perspective a plan."

Anne delivered her perspective: "There are huge deposits of stone made from differing geologic pressures on this lovely water-filled planet. There are more than enough to make possible the construction of edifices on each land mass where there are different tribes. The hominids would all focus these edifices towards their sun and star for they will have worked out that is where we come from. Maybe our geology engineer, Karl, could add more to my suggested erection of platforms using huge slabs of stone. These stones would be cut and carved into forms that fit together to form a platform.

"The tribes could be encouraged to climb up higher than the forest canopy to see their sun better from the enhanced elevation. One may ask why the need, or what incentive, for these primates to climb higher just to see the sky and sun."

Karl cleared his voice and caught everyone's attention. "I understand all that Anne has said, as well as what other members of this planning committee have contributed. From the original plan, I understood we would be interfering with fellow primates or hominids using genetic engineering to make them evolve into advanced civilized beings, more like us. It is understood that we must not just use them to reproduce ourselves by way of a surrogate system. If I am correct, we will place genes into their biology so that future generations will have some of our traits. What exactly are the traits that we will be passing over?

"Will it be our height, our physical strength, or our intelligence, or other physical attributes as well as mental capabilities of abstract thought and deduction?"

Karl spoke with a fierceness in his demeanour: "I know exactly what stone shape will be best for us to use and build. It would be more in the form of a triangle on one side, but putting four sides together to meet at one point. The next would be to use the local rock formations and to cut them into an exact replica of their star system. They have drawn stars that they see at nighttime in their caves, just as they have done with the animals they hunt for food."

Again he cleared his throat. "I have the dimensions as to how high and how big the base should be to hold the structure upright for a few thousand of their planet's years. I have drawn up plans, and as suggested earlier, we should have an educational aspect to our activities. For example, one full cycle of the year with the changing seasons equals three hundred and sixty-five days or one earth year. We should have exactly three hundred and sixty-five steps they could use to climb to the tops of these pyramids. These new tribes will be at such a height and angle that, using their sight, they will be able to calculate the rotations of their planet around the Sun and compare these with changes in weather cycles."

He lectured them, "So you see that from one building, they may be able, over time, to learn what a day is and be able to count the number of days in a full year. Indeed, everything could be explained through a knowledge structure that could be used to calculate differences such as the Sun as the centre of all their activities. Maybe in the future these hybrids with our genes and their primitive primate ones will turn their intelligence on and appreciate their role on this planet. In time they will see true north in the structure of the pyramid."

Karl had his structure. The historical fact bore a completely different outcome after hybridization of different genes. His pyramid stimulated a stream of events that was contrary to his wishful expectations.

# CHAPTER 13

# The Best-Laid Plans of Aliens and Earthlings

Speaking to the historical example of the 21ˢᵗ century, Les recalled, "In South America there is a pyramid that is called Tikal. Regardless of the noble intent of using these structures to improve mathematics and celestial knowledge, none of which happened, it was in fact a place where blood sacrifices were made. Cruelty prevailed as males were bled through a puncture made in their penis and the females bled from puncture of the tongue."

The Mayans used their power under separate leaders, called kings, whose role it was to maintain a balance of power. In fact, greed took over as they fought each other for wealth and territory. Modern-day archaeologists have recovered many of these beautifully formed pyramids. They noted all had three hundred and sixty-five steps to the top of the pinnacle, which made a terra year in days. However, instead of using it to see the wonders of the universe and of the Sun around which planet Earth revolved, it was used as a place for blood sacrifice. The pinnacle was so high that the stars and parts of the solar system could be seen and marvelled at the cosmos. This included cruelty as individuals were tossed down to their deaths to please celestial gods.

The Mayans were credited with the building of these wonders on the planet. In fact the Mayans evolved into a violent and savage society and almost self-destructed. One has to ask why.

Further discoveries revealed that these changes did not all occur because of the actions of male leaders. There is the tale of a female leader called Princess Six Sky. Modern-day anthropologists have recovered this tale from the carvings of a newly found pyramid. Essentially it states that there was a new dynasty formed around AD 40 or 50, and it is about a female leader.

She was both physically and mentally strong and was sent by her ageing father to a small city called Naranjo. It was there that modern-day archaeologists discovered a monument to this princess. The following incidents were carved in stone because on her arrival she laid out the following items to be tackled:

+ Having noted the power of agriculture in the survival of the working peoples, she directed water be brought to the fields where the people worked.
+ To ensure that the workers were well-fed, regular food was made available. Also, Princess Six Sky began to store excess food for the future so nutrition would always be available when times were bad.
+ Having had her trusted spies look at what other kings were doing, she came to the conclusion that they all had a political campaign to keep themselves in power. This gave her the information for her own leadership.
+ She bade her time until, around 761, all the kings were disposed of by their own hubris as only kings went to war

with their chosen families. The workers watched them march off. These kings killed each other off leaving a leadership gap.

Princess Six Sky had a son when she was around 19 years old. She protected him. When he was age 6, she placed him on the throne of a small city and made him king.

Over two hundred years of history were lost in this historical modern recount however, other cities were built, but to date in the 21st century, the recovery is still being done. These are listed to show the overwhelming power of construction that focused this population and allowed them to increase their numbers through better food. The question is, why did they feel the need to build these edifices? In the light of modern-day archaeology, it is a shame to think they were just seats of power and administration for an elite.

There must have been a significant reason for a spiritual, rather than a physical simplistic, show of power, although the power of humankind's ego has never failed to surprise anyone.

# CHAPTER 14

# Inscriptions on Ancient Cubes

"Cube number six is interesting, Dear," Les's wife, Alice, called out.

The old author enquired, "Why that particular block?"

"Well, you were looking for evidence of a deity earlier that would reveal whether aliens or ancients left messages or warnings for future generations to find. You also hoped that we would find some document describing explicitly the need for a deity," the grey-haired woman replied. She wore her glasses midway down her nose. She had a stack of loose papers in her hand and another sheaf on her desk in front of her.

Les coaxed her, "Go on, old thing! Do you have any evidence from your reading on what was meant or what you have interpreted from your search? What is the evidence?" The author was looking absent-mindedly at the old manuscript that lay open in front of him.

She answered, "Well! There is a reference to the philosophy of death on the cross. I believe these odd words appear to state,

'Redemption and salvation of humankind with the cosmos by the incarnate Son of God will occur after the general resurrection.' I believe that it implies the consequence: 'Death and destruction will be the permanent outcome.'"

Les, wearing his author's hat, replied, "Surely it suggests a deity that is God, who will look after the ills of the world. There must have been the belief in a Supreme Being or power that would solve all human woes. The cosmos filled that bill. Do you not think so?"

"It seems to fit the need. While the cosmos cannot be referred to as a 'being,' one cannot help but agree that it is what an all-powerful God could be. After all, it is power from the cosmos that has created everything we see and understand in the vastness of space and earth—and that includes ourselves," she quietly replied.

Les, coming closer to his pensive wife, said, "I would go even further, because there was a power that caused the cosmos to explode. You know that big bang thing? Those astrophysicists went crazy trying to explain why everything in the universe was 'created.' Now from a biblical perspective, God created the world and all therein. Yes, but why did he do that or feel the need to do such a thing? Humankind in fact is surely not the end result when compared with the grandeur of the cosmos. And who are we to question God anyway?

"So God from Genesis literature said, 'My time is immortal and endless. I will always have time for you,' or something to that effect.

"Well, this all-powerful God after the big bang must have had some leftovers, some end products of biological material. He used it to create humankind, but in his own image. Why? That I cannot fathom for surely he had many other choices, but he chose an image of himself. While this may sound like narcissism as in the Oscar Wilde play *The Picture of Dorian Gray*, surely the in-depth explanation must be related to spirituality and not come from the vanity of humankind's interpretation.

"Is there a broader context to the word *image* that would explain the love a human may have for another or for the beauty of land, forests, lakes, oceans and mountains, or for wild animals?" he asked.

"Well, that too may sound a bit too simplistic when the record, the Bible, does state that God is love," Alice replied.

Les said, "In that case, it is personification, which is beauty. *Love* is a word that means so many feelings, eh, part of that image?"

He continued: "Would the ability to reproduce the same species unblemished, like roses or hummingbirds, be in the image of a superior power or being?"

He thoughtfully continued, "I mean, to create a great red sequoia tree, I can understand—nay, comprehend—a bit of eternity or immortality from a simple perspective. Its life span records much of the physical evolutionary history of planet Earth over several centuries. Make it sentient, and one can have a pal for life and not have need of another presence for eternity. Humankind has become too troublesome and gets itself into problems. We then look up to the heavens, asking forgiveness for the mess we have made. Human beings never appear to learn from the spiritual support we receive after our physical mistakes, so we persevere like children, asking for God's assistance."

Alice said, "Are you becoming more facetious, even a bit more cynical, with each passing day? Maybe you should have a break from this project."

Les replied, "Sorry, Love! As I grow older, I feel the need for my old-fashioned religion; it comforts me. My parents set me up as a child to be a Christian, and while Sunday school cut into my playtime, it was a wonderful time where love surrounded me continuously in play and where I enjoyed the gifts arising from family life. Life was safe. It was a time when I had friends with whom I played and learned lots about my little world."

Alice interrupted him, saying, "So you chose to be a scientist, and that should have thrown out your historical beliefs about God and the Garden of Eden. Why did you not do that from a simply human perspective? Religion, based on Christian principles, asks humans to have faith because it goes against all logic and the laws of science. Besides, we speculate much more about the creations within the universe. There is no 'old man' lurking above the clouds of ferocious nucleic activity and listening to simple-minded biological beings called humans because he loves them."

"OK! OK! You have made your point." The old author laughed out loud. "My past will not leave me, even when my logical brain tells me such a belief is illogical. The difference is that I want to believe in God, an immortal being and the designer of the universe. The greatest power known to humankind is the cosmos, where there is expansion, so the stars are moving farther apart into endless space. Scientifically, there will be other big bangs in the empty expanses of space and time. If I am correct, then the present movement will be curtailed.

"You see, my love, I want the stars and their patterns to remain so our great-grandchildren will see them and marvel at their supernatural brilliance. Their presence will allow future generations' imaginations to grow and delight them until they choose what they want to do with their lives."

Alice said, "Now you are sounding like a besotted old fool, but I love this fool and do not want him to change. Come on! I have crumpets toasted and buttered. I will bring the honey." There was more laughter as two aged people sauntered out of the office towards the old sitting room that overlooked the garden and pool.

They sat down in the old comfortable leather chairs with cups of hot tea. "Ah! Chai-scented tea. Thank you, Love," Les whispered, his cup to his lips.

**A Wife's Soliloquy** – her husband left to go to the toilet -

Alice smiled at the man with whom she had lived for sixty-plus years. She marvelled at his still audacious enthusiasm for writing stories. She knew he was good at what he did, and she was satisfied with her own fulfilled life. The children had done what they'd wanted to do. They showed no enthusiasm to follow their professional scientist parents even though they had each done well in the sciences at university.

Alice was happy that Les had continued with his writing after he eventually gave up consulting for the lab supply companies. "Oh," she mumbled quietly. "The income was good, but it began to wear him down as new rules made visiting his clients and colleagues in the research labs difficult. His friend of fifty-plus years who owned the company understood. There was a good separation that assisted them to pay down the bank's line of credit, making it more manageable to live on our pensions.

"We had everything an elderly couple could desire, and while physical limitations hampered further travel for us outside the country, I told Les that he could go ahead on a cruise by himself because he needed to experience new geography. Such exposure seemed to stimulate his writing.

"He tried once going by himself and did not enjoy not having me beside him. I did not like the fact that he was on his own, so neither of us enjoyed being separated from the other. He never wanted to go without me again. I do not know why she had such apprehensions about travelling. I had become nervous and afraid of the whole prospect of going abroad.

"I chose to get involved in a passive way in his writing. I realized that he had ideas and imagination but no time to look up the little facts and bits he needed. He would call out, asking how to spell a word or for help to remember a phrase, the title of a play or an author from antiquity. He would ask, 'Can you look up where that information came from?' or 'Will you find the answer to a puzzle?' and a host of little things that would slow down his writing. He just wanted to get his thoughts or a sentiment that he had in mind down quickly, before he lost it, as he had said to me many times as if to justify his slowed memory.

"In fact, I did not mind searching for details, and in a strange way, I enjoyed looking up the obtuse details that seem to permeate his work. Oh, I never for once thought we would make any money out of this now really large library of books, thirty to date. 'Useful occupation,' he said so many times. 'It keeps dotage at bay.' We both laughed. But how true; we could both appreciate the joys of little things that were of interest to us. He would begin to spin a yarn, bringing us to laughter. Is that not really what real love and retirement is all about?

"Why did he receive this unusual stack of artifacts? What was it that our friend from the university appeared to want to avoid? If this is a scam or some prank, it is cruel. No! There is something unusual about how we got this ancient stuff. Over the years we have had gifts from friends and our daughters in appreciation for the gift of one of his books. It was treated as a lark and a reason for him to say, 'Let's go out and have a grand meal.' He'd take our family and friends out on short notice without ever thinking of the cost. The expense has never crossed his mind when he's wanted to take folks out for a grand old meal. It invariably ended up as being enjoyable. He said: 'If we had won the lottery millions, life could never be better. Invariably there would be a penalty to be paid for being rich without working for it.'

"'What kind of penalty?' I asked.

"'Look at all those who wanted fame and fortune. Invariably they lost a child, a teenager driving an expensive car, or else a grown-up or the kids became drug addicts or lost a spouse. There is always a penalty to be paid. Look at the movie stars of our day, eh!'"

\*   \*   \*

A hoarse voice interrupted. "Anyway, Sweetie, I believe in the translations we abstracted, even if they were misplaced as to what language was used in doing the translation."

Head down with a pensive look, Les quietly said, "We earthlings were given the gift of an evolutionary uplift, maybe through genetic engineering." He laughed at the irony should such a discovery be proven.

A shadow crossed the room. Alice and Les looked up briefly.

"Am I to assume that is a good thing?" Alice retorted, awaking from her private thoughts.

Les replied, "Ah! My dear, it is all perspective." He put on an Irish accent in jest. He continued, "You may have a point there. We both know, or knew, of certain individuals who have never evolved. They have remained unevolved and answer only by grunts and a limited vocabulary."

This was cause for more mirth as they recalled names of folks whose paths had crossed theirs. They laughed even harder when they focused on the politicians of the day.

# SECTION IV

# CHAPTER 15

# The Ancient Metallic-Covered Book

Author Les said, "Well, enough on these confounded cubes! I am tired of trying to read into the babble of Greek and Egyptian hieroglyphics and Mayan jabbering. Let us see what this wondrous bound text has hidden inside, ready for us. Will it reveal gems of hidden tales?"

He had the tiny brass key, now brown with age and dirt. He fitted it to the lock on the clamp, and much to his surprise it turned easily, not even a creak from the deposits on the exterior. As the brass-framed leather-bound cover opened, Les saw large cream-coloured pages written in black ink, probably using a feather quill. He spotted it right away. Suddenly he felt his eyes becoming heavy. He was alone and sat down with the text open on his desk in front of him. A shadow darkened the room.

As the old author's head bent and touched his chest, he heard a male baritone voice whisper gently into his mind. It was not unpleasant as he opened his mind as any old man would do. He just felt a nod coming on.

Interruption: "You who have opened this manuscript using the key are the chosen one. Pay no attention as to how you were chosen. In fact, no one chose you. You were among the few with knowledge and skill. We wanted someone to interpret why humankind has progressed relatively rapidly from an evolutionary perspective.

"The rough drawings you see of massive stones standing on their edges and in circles—if you measure them, you will find they were placed relative to the sun in its different phases. As a result, humankind came to understand the changes in weather on this planet. Secondly, if you articulate the times when seasonal changes alter, using the sundial you will find the best times to stimulate your agriculture initiatives for optimal growth. The weather will do its part in nurturing the growing sprouts and seedlings.

"Continue to use these physical celestial markings for the whole planet, and your education, with interpretation and understanding, will improve greatly throughout the farming sector of the planet. Similarly, you will see that in the most improbable of areas on the planet, we have used massive local rocks to erect buildings and to mark sites from which you can see the planets at night. Note their locations and compare them after making your own maps at different times of your three-hundred-and-sixty-five-day period. Complete the recordings for many years, and your knowledge of space and the cosmos will stimulate your imagination to unbelievable possibilities.

"I am Commander Sitla. Our race decided to remain on this planet after three generations in flight through the cosmos as our ship traversed the universe. Finding this solar system and this planet, blue because of water, and having such varied life forms, we decided it was time to end our long travel. Our new generation cautiously landed unobtrusively to study what life was like on this planet. There were no protests from any organized civilization. That was when I listened to the conversations of our youthful trained professionals. Throughout our journey, I placed myself into comas and timed my awakening after a new generation had grown up and been trained to take the place of deceased professionals."

Sitla continued, "I have learned from our ambitious scientists who exploited the opportunity to develop their disciplines. I could envisage the partial results of our intervention on your planet. The next decision we made was to enhance the genetic pool of the local primates that were evolving slowly through the system of natural selection. More importantly, the crew decided that we should not colonize the planet with only our Sig people. We stopped reproducing our species.

"We embarked on a plan to assist the primitive primate population by allowing them to observe our work and assist us in building the stone markers. These stone edifices were endowed with vital statistics of the planet's demographics. Next, the planting of native crops and the subsequent reaping of the harvests revealed a more efficient manner in the continuous cultivation of crops. Since Earth's progeny were ignorant and had no way of documenting what was going on, the next decision was to continue to add and improve on lasting indicators that would have longevity for your future edification. We began to teach the tribes the basics in using the resources that surrounded them."

The manuscript continued to speak: "Among the most important of these resources were the botanical species that were found in abundance. Our scientists made medicines that could protect the primates from the scourges of diseases and mini-epidemics that could have wiped the primates off the planet. We then embarked on simple agriculture that revealed non-meat protein food could be reproduced easily using benefits from the sun and rainfall. The remarkable result was the primates' rapid adoption of this learning, even in the first generation. They continued to improve, intensely so by the appearance of a third generation. Their lifetime was very short, less than three decades on Earth.

"At this early stage, your race needed to have comfort in what they were doing as our species began to slowly die off. Your first people noted their instructors were not seen as often and then not at all. We gave them the signal of the source of all power in the universe, which is the cosmos. However, we may not have done as good a job as we could, for they saw us return to our ship daily. This implanted in their simple mind the concept of a god or deity. They continued to look towards the skies and heavens and to call out to 'God' for assistance when they found themselves in difficulty. We continued to solve their petty problems, which further increased their dependency on their God.

"From this attempt to try to focus the population away from fighting and towards working together, they revealed a trait called 'love.' Such an emotion was not part of our genetic makeup. Their use of a deity that worked kindly and with consideration towards others was the result of love. It was not long after this that the shamans kept up the need for love to prevent fighting as a method of settling disputes. That aspect took over, and a few decades later they began to use their brains more fully and to rationalize life. However, the leaders of their spiritual endeavours, whom we had ignored as being harmless to our mission, started expanding profound philosophies based on love."

The manuscript voice spoke, "The basic template was very much the same, but we did not count on your species being able to use these different philosophies to band into groups of similar minds and then follow one or the other teaching. It was the first attempt to get a majority of followers to believe in one shaman's fact over another. The rivalry was gentle to begin with, but it soon was compounded by the killer instinct to gain a majority of people on the one side. Strange to us that these wise shamans preached that there could be only one true religion. This was the beginning of keen rivalry over religious beliefs. We are a long-lived race, in fact four to five times your own life span.

"Throughout the centuries following, this rivalry of religions was the cause of much conflict. Many lives were lost because of the extreme positions taken by each of the different philosophies. We looked on in a bemused state to see how it would all work out. Essentially, it ended in their wanting to know which one god (us) favoured the children of this planet. Your society remained in this simple phase for far too long. We did not favour any one tribe or clan over the other; that was strictly your species' dictate.

"Wars were waged, lasting for long periods of time, and were fought over the philosophy dictates. Many innocents perished. Observing from the disputes, we deduced that 'bad' individuals of your species used this 'good' to do evil on their behalf. We inserted genes that should have encouraged growth and brain development. The intent was for your species to survive celestial and Earth's physical upheavals. Again your primitive mind interpreted such natural attacks as the displeasure of God.

"We did not foresee, or understand, when your species chose to select genetic traits such as cruelty, lust and greed as part of the new reproductions. These were brought to the forefront by tribal fighting. These manifestations frightened our species, a non-aggressive race in the cosmos. Intellectually observing, and through discourse for the first time, we began to study the cause and effect of these traits and the reasons for them to exist. This is where, in the absence of knowledge or experience, the intellect returns to philosophy. While such a hypothesis does not give answers readily, it allows for broader speculation on behaviour.

"We left the aggressive gene, in the event that it may prove necessary for your species' defence against alien attacks in the future. However, when your citizens began to form nations, we lacked the foresight to see that this would encourage massive wars and loss of life. Your rapid development and ability to create weapons of mass destruction for use against your own species was a lesson we learned after interacting with your species.

"The reason for documentation of these facts was to explain that we, an advanced civilization, embarked on this project with good intentions. We had never known aggression in our evolution millions of your years earlier, while your planet was still being formed from the energy outbursts that brought the cosmos into existence. You will work this out in the future.

"I, Commander Sitla, conclude this report and admit that a number of our workers did mate with your species, so hybrids exist in your population. I set up an enquiry into why some of our species had reproductive sex with your species. It was revealed that your female species were found to have a natural sensual talent in carnal knowledge that attracted our males, but later on our females also followed with your males. This most attractive feature was circulated to all members of our species in our crew, many of whom were our non-scientific workers. They were not scientists or engineers, but they worked as assistants to our lead hands. As a result, many of them could imitate what their lead hands did.

"To be honest, while we allowed our worker force of thousands aboard the ship to land and remain as long as they wanted, there were no limitations as to what they should do. A few of our female species tried to learn what your females could do so easily. In spite of our physical differences in size, our females did mate with your males and had offspring, who now exist in your population.

"Our females never had the experience of sex as physical enjoyment, whereas both sexes of your species do. Another new experience was the feeling of pain during delivery of the newborn infant. Our Sig females explained that conception had brought them physical pleasure, even though pain was new to them. Their large wombs allowed for easier delivery. They all reported that once they had completed the delivery and saw the fine features of the newborn, they had no regrets and would repeat the whole rebirth process again.

"Our crew knew that this was the final stop in our long but tedious journey through the cosmos. They knew they would never remain alive if we were to undertake a return journey to our planet. They experimented and explored the physical pleasures of primitive living and also assisted in building markers to leave the footprint they once knew on planet Sig. Strange, though, many crew members wanted to live amidst a simple family unit and remain close to the villages and growing townships. In contradiction, our workers enjoyed recreating the structures of planet Sig.

"I also allowed these structures to be built beneath the great oceans on this planet so that a good many of our crew members could continue their lives as a Sig society away from the new populations of earthlings. Only a select few leaders in my crew knew of my plans to enter the second dimension of space. Few commanders had that privilege or the knowledge to do so. Since I was responsible for the crew, I had to make this division as the majority of our workers loved staying in this solar system. To many it was their home. They knew nothing of planet Sig; it was just a history lesson for them as many were born in transit. Now they had a family that was tied to a solid reality, not that of being born on a spaceship and seeing just one physical type of being.

"It would have been unwise to take them into an environment that was still unknown to us. Therefore, the decision for them to remain was completely out of my hands. I had done what I suspect many commanders might have attempted somewhere else in the universe. The whole idea of happiness was observed by members of your early race, who smiled easily and laughed when they had food and health. Your early ancestors were travelling around the planet, across huge frozen expanses that linked together the non-aquatic surfaces that you call continents. The time frame, if you were to use the technology of deterioration of carbon in organic forms, would be around thirteen thousand of your years ago.

"You will observe that we continued to use stone released to our dimensions by cutting lasers, from mountains and igneous rock eruptions from ground near the volcanoes. Using antigravity strips, as well as our own musculature and large size, we moved the large carved building stones to the sites where the pyramid structures were to be erected. The natives accepted our structures because our method was similar to theirs when making tools out of stones.

"They were also quick learners and copiers of our technology of building, as seen when they began to use stone to build their own homes. This meant that they would no longer seek refuge in the caves and caverns, where there was limited protection from weather and attacks from the animal world. We also showed them how to keep a water supply close, by damming small streams, which could be used when there was drought. We did not pass along our high-tech equipment and went to great lengths to keep it hidden. We had to make sure they did not know of the technical power we had.

"These early tribes were slender of build with straight noses, unlike the primitive tribes in the tropical parts of the planet who had broad noses. We called them 'Clovis' because of the specific stone tools they made."

The strong voice continued to speak to the sleeping author: "It was a footnote in one of our reports that many of the hybrids began to construct their own designs of pyramid structures. However, archaeological evidence revealed that they lacked the engineering finesse. These structures now defile the landscape as deteriorating piles of stone and mud in deserts. Even if they could cut the full stone block, they could not move the block because they did not have either the manpower or the antigravity power. As a result, they made their homes from smaller blocks of stone, which could be rolled using a pool of manpower. This posed a limitation as to the height of their structures."

# CHAPTER 16

# The Manuscript Reports No Need for Interpretation

"Unknown documenter, to me long dead, at least in this cosmos, I do not know what will happen when the few of us leave for the second dimension. You are tasked with summarizing our presence here and all we have intervened in to advance your society. Our scientists saw your future evolution, and it is only fair that such a tale should be reported to your civilization. In your early evolving civilization, all your tribes were exposed to dangers from the geologic settling down of the planet. This was easily discovered judging by the number of volcanoes that allowed internal explosive heat from the planet's core to be released. The force from deep within erupted without notice to your tribes, coming from the shifting plates that cover your planet.

"The next danger came from large fauna that were still evolving as well. These can be seen in our etchings left on the enclosed cubes. You will label them as cave bears, mastodons, elephants, bison and sabre-toothed cats. They would just as easily attack and eat the hunted as they would be eaten by the hunters. The Clovis had a stable genetic past, and we thought it better to work with this tribe on your planet.

"It worked well. After gene insertion, the next generation phenotypically appeared to have increased intelligence by our measurements, and that was a practical precaution. They were a more 'thinking before acting' group, and there was a gentleness in their physical appearance that was deceiving.

"They also appeared to be healthier on the new diet of both animal and plant protein that included seeds and cooked grasses at an earlier age. However, the first genetically enhanced tribes remained very much at the hunting-gathering phase of development for a few more generations. When we compared them with the indigenes moving from the northern part of the continent, we found there were no genetic similarities other than they were primates. These indigenes from the north were heavy-browed with a rough-faced demeanour and hard, round heads.

"Our anthropologists found that the Clovis, in comparison, had a more evolved DNA profile, but their physical makeup remained short of protein. This is an important part in the concept of evolution as stated before. Cosmogenesis as a phenomenon is described as being under the power of cosmic forces. It is what was responsible for the formation of the inanimate world and its evolution. It is not entirely the same for the life of a 'primate being' with the potential to travel across the cosmos."

Commander Sitla's voice was real to the old author, who remained asleep but who was listening to the full story that was written in Sanskrit, which he was unable to read, but it was being read to him from the ancient book he had opened. He was alert but incapable of movement. However, he was aware that he was listening to a story in his head. This was not an unusual state for him as an author. It was how he was able to produce his 30 novels, all of which were designed in his head.

Les thought to himself, *Yes, I wrote from different parts of the planet where a combination of spiritual truths and locations would mysteriously enter the story after I was writing for long hours. The story would unfold in a way I did not expect, and I had no knowledge of how it would end.*

"This is the unheard mystery of writing novels," he whispered to himself.

Comfortable in the knowledge, as this was a natural state for him, Les closed his eyes and listened.

"The primate life on the planet fifteen thousand years earlier already showed signs of having power over parts of the environment. It was not a false abstraction to prognosticate these primates would dominate all other life forms on the planet. Our scientists were completing works on the southern continents, which had different climate zones, of which a large part was in the tropical regions. They noticed a change from the rich green foliage to flora that had started to become desertified.

"The land had grown the same wheat for many years, but in the absence of moisture and under the intense rays of the sun, the land had become arid. The Clovis witnessed early brown-skinned primates who were smaller in stature and were having a problem in handling their survival.

"On the other hand, while still in the tropical zone, primates had begun to wander into lusher surroundings, following the shores of the large southern oceans. As they travelled, these groups found food that was easily obtainable along the shoreline. Using their methods of gathering shelled sea animals, they stopped travelling and settled down, building early villages. Others continued to move eastward along the oceans' shores and across large land masses. These land masses were under the continual shifting tectonic plates as the planet cooled down.

"Land masses began to separate as the covering tectonic plates shifted, separating one land mass from the other. As a result of the climate changes that followed, both flora and fauna continued in a parallel but separate phenotypic evolution. Because these primates had settled down, had come together to form families and then had formed organized groups, there was the beginning of intelligence. It appeared as if the whole group became one thinking organism. Our evolutionary scientists had observed similar behaviour in flocks of birds and in schools of fishes in the oceans.

"This was a new observation, but it appeared that the same might be happening with the primate species. This would present a grave danger to the planet should primates begin to work as one brain without thought.

"It was also the beginning of a phenomenon called oogenesis, which is the formation of human thought. However, this human evolution included the need for a power or deity that helped to stabilize society, the beginning of the spiritual state of humankind that you modern species understand. You will now find that the shortcoming of this philosophy is a two-edged sword that does not always serve the generic good.

"That is all for now, old scholar. However, if you go to the end of this historical record, the last two pages will give you an insight into the future of the peoples on your planet. How we have done this remains a mystery to me. I would like you to think of us as not interfering but as a kindly race wanting to do the right thing. Try to understand, we do not know of other primates similar to us in the cosmos at the time of our existence. We were lonely and wanted companions; hence, the writing on the blocks or cubes is a historical account using your beautiful languages.

"Final note: Old scholar, know that we are heading into the second dimension and may not be able to return to this dimension. We have left cosmic clues as to what we have done, should another ship from planet Sig arrive to investigate this quadrant in the future. They should have my log reports, which would have taken several light years to return to Sig. Those already in transit elsewhere in the universe might not have been able to collect these logs. They will have a complete history of this pioneer effort. Commander Sitla out for the last time."

## The Last Pages Unfold

"Humankind seeks out the caryatides, which are the statues of Olympia. Your early cities had a great number of key factors that reveal the emancipation of human thought unblemished. Seek the wisdom from Amphipolis in the ancient Greek ruins. Some information is not quite accurate. For instance, there are thirteen constellations, not twelve as the early Greeks stated. Then again they did not have our technology to see first-hand what is in the cosmos. Note their marker, Ophiuchus the serpent bearer, the last two months of your year, which should reveal something about planet Sig, which has a utopian civilization."

# CHAPTER 17

# The Cosmic Mystery of Humankind

"It is a message explaining that humankind is immortal, although not in the human flesh, which lives on borrowed time. That external clothing called the flesh will die and decay. The immortal part of humankind is its soul or spirit, spawned from the all-powerful Being that started the big bang and guided the formation of the universe. It has to return as energy from whence the spirit originated!" shouted the old author to his wife, Alice.

Alice responded, "Now that will explain what the last mystery of the cube/block has revealed. I cannot wait to hear what you have found."

The author said to her, "Really, Love, it has been in front of us all the time, and it lies in a religious philosophy of our Christian religion. Why have we not understood it after a lifetime of searching quietly in our souls and spirits?"

Alice said, "I must admit a great many things in life are only revealed when the time is appropriate. We were not ready in our youth or middle age to grasp its significance. If we had had such an understanding, how could we have changed our direction in living out the rest of our lives?"

Les replied, "You have a point there. Maybe we are not expected to understand such a mystery. Why are we only here for a short time when our purpose is to improve the lot of humankind by millimetres in our evolution, compared with the distances and workings of the cosmos? If we had that knowledge in advance, then it would have stymied the direction we (as individuals) had started to carve from our experiences, our work and our connections with others in daily contact, as well as our comprehension."

Alice, in a firm voice, retorted, "Hold on! I do not much like the idea of a philosophy that dictates a preplanned destiny. While I do agree we make our own destiny, while we live day to day we respond to our surroundings and its demands, and we make choices. Does that mean that some great force makes us respond to a designed behaviour?"

The author said, "Well, I see where you are going. If we follow your outlook, it would lead to a fatalistic conclusion. The prime example being, the murderer could say, 'It was my destiny' or 'God made me do it.' That would really ruin the rule of law that has evolved as civilized behaviour in a civilized society."

There was a pause as the two mature individuals sitting in the little cluttered office reminisced. They had performed this ritual for many years, sipping hot Earl Grey tea and letting thoughts of their past experiences come together to make some sort of sense.

Les said, "You see, Love, we may have indeed been doing that anyway because we, in the Christian philosophy, follow the Ten Commandments as a guide to our behaviour in our society. Would that not be considered an interference by an immortal in the lives of human beings, in fact one that could lead us to a fatalistic, albeit practicing, healthy good behaviour?"

"I see your point in that explanation, but the same could be said about our education and cultural diversity," Alice responded. "Not that we sorry non-practising Christians follow a routine of supplication daily as the people of non-Christian religions do by breaking the day's routine to perform the rituals of thanking God for guidance and wanting us non-believers to live by their rules."

"Then our upbringing, regardless of our religion, our education or our practices in society, has combined to pollute the inherent belief that comes from the purity and creation of the cosmos."

Alice, yawning, said, "Well, all this discussion is great, but what did the last cube reveal based on all our digging around in human activity since the beginning of time?"

Author Les, in a distracted tone, replied, "You may be right, but there is still much to understand and abstract. The last block shows the limitation of where religious philosophy has directed us." This was followed by a long pause.

Then Les began his diatribe: "Our Catholic Church preaches the concept of transubstantiation, which is the conversion of simple bread and wine into the flesh and blood of our holy Saviour Jesus Christ. Yes indeed, many practitioners of our religion appear to get peace of mind from the distractions of the world by this indulgence of faith. They and their families have, by adhering to this religious routine on Sunday, and maybe for the older generation every day, as it was when I was young, found peace.

"That ritual in itself is a good thing. Others believe that through this weekly practice, the 'goodness' of the Saviour reaches down, forgiving them of their past transgressions, so they have a clean slate (or conscience) to begin living their lives in the turmoil that is life all over again.

"Having lived a relatively safe life in a Judeo-Christian country for most of our lives with our family, we have seen that the population has followed the rules of civility. So the question I ask is why these congregations return the next week to confess their sins to the Father before they take their communion. What could they have done so sinful in a week?

"The point, maybe, is that there are different types of sins, such as bad thoughts or pining for a friend's wife or husband, and I suppose others such as swearing using God's name.

"These sins seem so trivial. As long as no others have been hurt, does God really need to hear them? At my age, I think it is an utter waste of God's invaluable time. He needs all his time to continue building the great cosmos and allowing other bioforms to evolve to a better stage. Humans may be just a trial run of his creation that needs improvement. Let's face it, we are a deplorable mob really, aren't we?"

Alice listened and nodded. "I do not know. I should have spent more time reading up on what is it that God wants of us. Surely swearing and lust for all sorts of things is in reality pretty petty for the Great Creator of humankind to forgive. Or is the human still on trial after using our free will inappropriately?"

Les replied, "You know, from my teenage education through my Jesuit teachers, the suggestion is that my conscience should tell me good from bad. If I choose to ignore my conscience, I pay the consequence under the laws of humankind and society. God has forgiven whatever transgressions I may have made anyway, as any understanding father would do, do you not agree?"

Alice, looking at the clutter on her desk, mumbled, "I am not agreeing to any such thing. You have thrown that stuff at me over the years. Why in the name of God did that Catholic philosophy become so ingrained in you? I know, it was classical conditioning that those priests used on vulnerable innocent youthful minds, wasn't it?"

## A Fleeting Break in Time

The author quietly reminisced. "My old mentor of my teenage years, Father Harkins, at Lady of Fatima College, tried to explain this to me when I was at the age of nineteen. I had read the catechism books and the satellite readings that he provided to my friend and me so we could take our vows as Catholics. Please remember, I have been a Christian all my life, but in the Presbyterian Church. I changed direction after attending a Catholic private college paid for by my father. Strange that neither my father nor my mother dissented at my conversion. In fact, they said nothing when my other brothers and sisters did the same over the years.

"I did not seek to know why or ask why they behaved in such a way. I didn't even ask, 'No response then?' It was only when I was in my sixth decade that I asked the question, long after their deaths. Strangely, I do not understand what wisdom really is. It was gleaned from their many letters to me as a young man settling down to married life in a new country. Their love for their eldest son surpassed the trivial and manifested itself many years later, I know now, having reread their now ancient letters. Strange, even at that time when I needed understanding, it took a close colleague to point out that fact to me. It happened after I had showed him the letters and my parents' response when there was a revelation about my past supposed 'misbehaviour.'

"I did not carry any guilt with me for I had already told everything of my past to my future wife when we first met. The purpose was to prevent any mishaps from the past that might interfere with our future after the children had left home.

"To my always beautiful wife, your unusual mind knew how to kindly interpret behaviors in both our pasts. Living together, one shares so many things and great insights are discovered together. I believe it is because we discuss and thus understand, then accept, the frailty of human behaviour and thus our own."

Alice interrupted Les to say, "Please continue with the supposed interpretations you uncovered. You appear to have drifted away. Where were you for the last few minutes? You were muttering to yourself."

"Yes! Yes! The explanation of transubstantiation is what I was trying to recall, and I found that it was described in the Greek Orthodox scriptures in Genesis. There was a description in the Catholic teachings, but the Greek appeared clearer to me: 'As our humanity assembles the material world, there is Eucharistic transformation.' It continues, explaining that the 'totality of the world and the duration of Creation become consecrated into "One."

"Why is that so profound?" Alice asked. :It is accepted religious Christian dogma or philosophy. I do not see the breakthrough you have made with cube 12."

Les replied, "Well, it happened when I was having a sip of my coffee this morning. I learnt that there is a metaphysical or supernatural component to human existence that will never be understood by scientists. Scientists deal with the laws of science that they have created to explain physical laws in the universe. In fact, Dear, scientists deal in speculations on the creation of the universe.

"However, religious philosophy does explain that 'oneness' implies that after death, the spirit returns to the cosmos from which it was loaned to us living things/beings on planet Earth for a limited time.

"In biblical philosophy, especially when taken from Greek Orthodox literature, it is explained that there is a pinnacle in spiritual evolution referred to as Point Omega. It explains the supreme synthesis of the spirit in terms of an evolutionary goal. When humans reach that point, the phenomenon is similar to death. As I tried to explain earlier, in reality it is a simple metamorphosis and accession to the supreme synthesis with the cosmos."

There was a long silence between the two old scholars before it was broken by Alice: "Is that supposed to give us a better understanding of what happens after we die? I suppose it is as good as anything." She was muttering to herself, but the old man was listening. "It will give peace to the mind before we give up, knowing we will be returning to something from which we came. *Yes,* that is comforting."

Les had been up most of the night dealing with every possibility, so he was mentally satisfied at this stage when his enthusiasm was awakened. It was possible that later on he might have lots of questions, but right now he was leaving the right-brained individual, his wife, to process his findings.

Les, wearing the author's hat, thought to himself, *However, major unanswered basic problems still remain as to who sent these artifacts to me. Of more importance, what will happen after solving the puzzles? What am I supposed to do with the answer?*

A smile crossed his aged face. Suddenly a thought dawned on him: all that he was doing was collecting this information for one of his books. He would leave interpretations for others to ruminate over long after he has gone. His own philosophy, he was convinced, was that he would join the power in the cosmos, knowing that in some form he would return.

His smile broadened as his fingers moved over the keyboard. "I will never get used to speaking to that software to commit to writing my stories. It is better for me to type using my fingers."

# CHAPTER 18

# Introspection of an Aged Commander

"It is my desire that while we are training and teaching these evolving primates, we implant genes selected by our geneticists and remove unsuitable genes at conception in their females. The hybrids born should be closely monitored throughout their relatively short lives. As the environment may play a part in an individual, genetic behaviour should be adjusted to accommodate their savant behaviour by one of our caretakers.

"They already are in awe of our ability in using advanced technology (unseen by them) to build the indicator rock buildings. It is our hope that these edifices should remain as examples for them to replicate in their own villages, in mini towns and eventually in cities to house thousands more of their populace. By our providing the technique of rotating crops that continues to provide a stable food supply, they will become self-sufficient. They should also be taught to maintain a regular dependable food source through storage bins and clean water from their pure mountain snowfall.

"The end result is that they rely only on themselves, having total control of these vital resources. Already we have seen they are beginning to settle down from a nomadic life. The leader chosen by us will take credit because he was shown how to relate natural changes in the environment as the sun undergoes its rotations at different times of the year.

"We must teach the leader or shaman to learn the basics about medicinal plants that are plentiful in the surrounding forests. In that way he will treat simple illnesses in their families, and this will impose a dependency from the masses on their healers.

"Under no circumstance should any of our crew allow them to look at us as deities or as gods. Explain that we come from a planet across the vast empty space called the cosmos. When they are ready to travel into this empty space, they will find us on our home planet. By then, they will have depleted their Earth of all its mineral wealth. They will recognize the massive riches to be taken from the empty planets, huge asteroids and comets present in large amounts throughout the universe above their heads. When earthlings eventually learn to travel into space, they will be on their own."

Commander Sitla reminisced: "We hope that humankind will understand that the world around them is in a continuous state of flux. Physical changes will be radical to their newborn appearance, although some will not see the differences because it will be in their genetic map. It may show in intelligence not so easily observed or measured, but the hybrid psyche will be more difficult to understand. Humankind has used brute force to fight for power over other people before our intervention. That power will change and become more secretive and cunning as they continue to evolve.

"While we do not understand in what form the primitive killer gene will manifest itself, one can only surmise it will show as simply a desire to master the weaker human. The male of the species likes, in his primitive mind, to own many females and to have many offspring as was observed by Sitla's anthropologist scientist studying the massive great apes in the forests. The superficial interpretation was a desire to pass along his genes to future progeny. This state might continue for many hundreds of Earth years; however, the female humanoid species, unknown to her biology, will choose the next fertilized egg and the spermatozoon that will be the fertilizer.

"Where did this selective force originate? Was it for a better offspring, or was there another reason, something that might bring about a balance of power for the 'helpless' female? Our anthropologists working with our geneticists made such a deduction by studying the great mammals on Earth.

"The desire for power and control will increase abnormally in a few leaders. Their primitive cunning will allow them to invite clan members to form large armies. They will build new weapons and use wild steeds to cover greater territory. Getting into other human villages and cities, they will attack and dominate their neighbours. In doing so, they will improve their wealth by taking away livestock, male youths to be used as slaves, and females to be used as broodmares. Man's inhumanity to man will follow for thousands of years.

"We had hoped that with increased knowledge they would change or that the change period would be shortened and humankind would treat their species more kindly. This will not happen for many generations.

"There will be mutations in future generations when the brute within will be curtailed to some extent and a younger generation will speak openly of the power of love. Love will conquer in the end as they will show the ability to love opposite sexes and similar sexes. Unusual reproductions will be incapable of reproducing. They will have a life of total carnal pleasure. There will be very smart and intelligent reproductions in the new hybridized species; on the other hand, there will be fools and physically abnormal mutations.

"Humankind, the enhanced primate, must adapt to these biological changes for the good of their evolved society. There must be accommodations through reformation of policies as the demand for inclusiveness will grow. In such adapting and making of accommodations, human beings will come to the decision that they have no choice but to live in harmony with different individuals who have different opinions and cultures.

"Professional staff, we hope, will teach by example, so we built edifices around different non-aquatic areas as in the forests and deserts and also in the temperate climates. It was our hope to show them how to harness the waters from the rivers to assist them in building and maintaining a simple agrarian economy. Fresh water tumbling from the mountains' heights, from melting snow, they have used in the past for washing themselves in the rivers daily. Those tribes that lived close to rivers and seas exploited aquatic life forms, catching them for food. They appeared to need flesh protein in their diet, and we have observed their brain tissues require a high-protein diet to develop."

## The Philosophical Argument

"Primitive primates should not be helped or be protected from their hunting and gathering skills for they need this activity to thrive and learn from their mistakes. If they are helped, they will become accustomed to living comfortably and will lose the ability to survive. There is a vital need for challenge as part of their evolution. We understand what is needed for their survival and did not interfere as they learnt through experience of hardships. When unforeseen forces from weather and the physical environment occur, the primal need to survive will take over.

"Our scientists also studied the physical history of this planet. Our geologic surveys revealed massive flooding, fierce wintry storms and tropical storms where lightning caused fires and volcanic eruptions caused havoc to all life forms of this planet. This has been the history of the planet, and it appears it will be a permanent feature in the foreseeable future.

"Earthquakes and erupting volcanoes, both on land and under the oceans, must be experienced to allow humankind to understand these potential catastrophes. Members of my spaceship, *do not make the mistake of intervening to help them.* They must learn to survive on their own, and that will mean loss of life. But they have a high degree of emotion that binds them together into families and clans. This is a good trait for them to build larger settlements and townships. There will be the need to learn to obey the leader or chief of their choice.

"Their lesson is in how to become adaptable to changes beyond their control. They must do this on their own without our assistance. They must learn to live in a world of continual change that will surround them all the days of their lives. One day in the future, they will all perish on this planet and in this solar system, but we should have left them with enough information to look after themselves. In searching for their past, they will build a great future based on intelligence. I understand that a number of our crew would prefer to remain and die on this planet.

"There will be hybrids in the new generation with just enough intelligence and physical features to leave a faint imprint of our presence.

"Humans will not notice the physical differences that will take place in the outlying areas, such as where the black skins and island populations reside. Any physical trait that is ours, such as a thick neck, will disappear."

Such were some of the final thoughts of alien Commander Sitla.

# CHAPTER 19

# What Do These Cubes Tell Us?

Les the author said, "It was the ancient Greek philosophers who first made that comment, so what is it doing on an alien cube, I wonder?

"A cultural implant states that nothing will remain constant but that everything will change, so humankind has to get used to that fact. Scientists state that the whole cosmos began with a big bang, and humanity at the time believed this explanation, which is as incongruous as saying that a powerful individual or spirit came and created the earth. However, everything is plausible, and to more than a few, the Creator of the cosmos built a garden then placed all animal and plant kingdoms into it, along with humankind. This did not mean that humankind would have an easier life on the planet on which they live with limited skills needed to survive. There had to be an internship period as the planet took on the role of teacher."

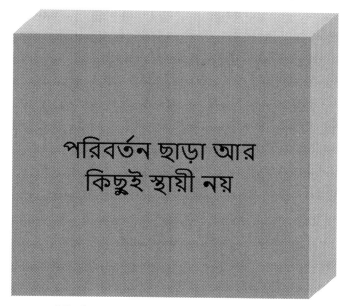

Nothing is permanent except change.

Les continued: "Whether it was a big bang or a creation from the original basis, nothing resembled the same as what was present at its beginnings. These words bear a truth. If we look around us, we can see from childhood experiences and from those of our grandchildren that nothing is the same. Thank goodness for change; it is the only way to human evolutionary progress. Yes, my grandson listened when I told him of my school days. When I misbehaved, I would be whipped. Yes, in one or two generations, many social ills were taken as the wisdom of that age.

"His remark was, 'Why did you not dial 9-1-1?' When I told him we did not have a telephone, that in fact there was only one for the street—and besides, kids were not allowed to use the phone—he thought Granddad was telling him a frightening story.

"Yes, within such short a time, many social changes have made life better. A few of my colleagues who study human evolution told me that humans use their inherent facial twitches to communicate sympathy and understanding to other humans. The face actually has metamorphosed to show non-verbal responses, but of a deeper emotional understanding. It appears that human societal growth and brain enhancement over the generations has effected physical changes. Will our brain one day be awakened and be able to transmit thoughts to another non-verbally, I wonder?"

"What are you thinking of that has that insipid grin on your face?" came the voice of Les's wife, Alice, who was carrying a tray of tea and scones.

"Hello, Dear! Ah! Tea time break. Is it strawberry jam or peach?" Les turned from his desk to assist in clearing a spot to place their tea. The old couple settled down to sip their mugs of hot tea. Slowly a scone was lifted to the mouth, eyes closed. The tidbit melted in the mouth as the sugared fruit brought out more saliva than was necessary to digest the comforting morsel. There was no need to rush or to do anything other than what these two enjoyed doing.

"In response to your question, I was recalling, in our eight decades of existence, how many social changes have taken place. Whether or not they were good or bad, life for individuals, regardless of where one lives on this planet, has changed in six decades. Society has never stood still but continually moves ahead with each generation regardless of economic wealth. Yes, even today folks argue about the different political leaders and what they stand for, but in reality these individuals' purpose is to turn the wheel of society forward."

"From the outside looking on dispassionately, not being part of the political system, you are correct." His wife continued holding her mug and sitting back in her office chair.

"It has come to my mind, since we are dealing with abstract thoughts that I do not believe they knew it was part of their destiny in performing that task. I mean, we may use the word *legacy* for what they might have achieved during their tenure, but they were really adding a minute step to the evolutionary changes that would have taken place anyway."

"Exactly!" exclaimed the author, glad to get the support of his companion. "It has happened during our brief time on earth. Just look at what has happened in sixty years of history. Now that is exciting. Just think what massive changes will take place in the future. That is a prospect worthy of some thought, isn't it?" said the excitable Les.

# CHAPTER 20

# Truth amidst Satire—a Human Trait

The author said to his spouse, "You know, Love, there is an old translation of the thoughts and philosophy of Lucretius. Yes. It was a scholar from either Oxford or Cambridge who did the heavy work of trying to interpret these advanced thoughts on science. It was published and left to languish in the old book section of that horrible bookstore run by a beastly Jewish woman. She made a fortune exploiting the hard work and hours of toil of many authors with her promises to sell their books. None of these authors ever made significant income to have a good life, and she had the audacity to recommend which books to buy."

Les stuttered as he usually did when he was emotionally aroused. "With such nepotism, she allowed only a few of her close friends to prosper. I know, when one of my books was given to her establishment to be sold, it lasted less than a day on the front shelves before being cast into the dollar bin."

Alice smiled, her head bowed. "Do not become bitter. It is just business, and you are not amongst those who will butter up individuals in the author community. You therefore pay the price for your exclusive behaviour, and you always will." Thoughtfully, his wife continued to show support. "You of all people should know that where there is nepotism, there is no room for logic or fairness. In fact, the bookseller's method of operation only worked partially, unbeknown to her. She might have missed out on many good books that would have made even more profit. However, she, like all business people, looks at things simply as the next dollar with limited insight into the potential millions that may be in the offing if a little thought for others were given limited priority."

Les nonetheless continued, "Furthermore, I do not believe she had ever read any of the books. She had a number of young university females whom she lorded over who did the reading and made their recommendations. She then recommended Book of the Month, so a lucky friend author of hers received a burst of funds to continue with the worthwhile profession of writing. Really, I am just a bit jealous."

Les turned to his desk. "Back to science, as that is the only world where truth and honesty share an ethical advantage. For example, this was one of the first scientific interpretations left to us on earth and attributed to a science scholar. Who in creation had such foresight and practical knowledge in the days of yore? Better still, how did they achieve such wisdom?"

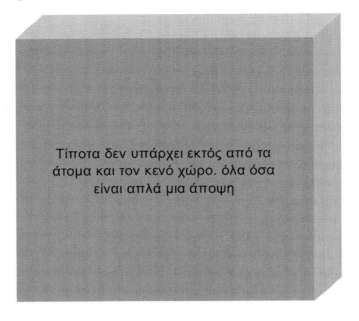

Τίποτα δεν υπάρχει εκτός από τα άτομα και τον κενό χώρο. όλα όσα είναι απλά μια άποψη

Nothing exists except atoms and empty space; everything else is just an opinion.

—Democritus

Alice replied, "You must stop putting a bite on your words when individuals disagree with your outlook and philosophy. It will turn you into a bitter old man. You are better than that, you know!"

Les said, "From that old blue-covered paperback book on our bookshelf, very wise words and concepts were translated long before Einstein's mathematical mumbo-jumbo and that stuff about matter and the universe. Here were words written by a being who had practical knowledge of that truth long before it was written."

Silence fell. Alice quietly examined the cube and the Greek writings. Musing, she thought, *He is telling the truth. He understands the depth of thought, that man of mine with an intellect I will never understand.*

Les began speaking: "Hypothetically, do you think it may be

possible that a being appeared on this planet long before we, as an evolving race, knew anything and left these gems for us? Alternatively, there must have been a part of human evolution when a much more advanced civilization existed that has now has completely vanished. Maybe before the Great Flood, some advanced atheist mind may have existed."

Alice, looking at the old bent figure sitting with his head down, offered, "You are getting close to the truth, aren't you?"

Les, looking up at his wife, smiled as though coming out of a trance. "Maybe, my dear. Just maybe."

Alice, thinking as befitted her quiet disposition, soliloquized to herself: *Such tremendous knowledge accumulated over decades stored between his large ears. Therein lies a brain led by the unbelievable imagination of a very unusual man. I have lived with him for many years and still do not understand his enthusiasm, which has never dropped, for living happily. Give him an idea for an occasion, and he immediately jumps into action with a plan and then goes overboard. Of course, everything he proposes never has a limit on resources or spending. He always had confidence.* "We will get on top of our line of credit and leave a bit more money for our kids. Never worry."

Author Les spoke out: "There is a lot more evidence of languages and etchings on tablets in caves and other places that have been removed, only to remain in dusty museums, none of them being deciphered. Why should I try to interpret these artifacts when professionals could not interpret them? This is another waste of time. The reader of non-fiction will not be impressed, although I believe he will catch the gist of what I am getting at."

Alice said, "What is another example of an etching that cannot be interpreted, besides those of the Mayans and those on the backs of the big heads left on Easter Island?"

Les replied, "Yes, I wish to get away from the Egyptians, the Mayans and the Easter Island great stones, as well as Stonehenge. Do you know when the Brits began digging up the whole island during the period of great archaeological discovery, there was another group working on the islands northeast of Scotland? They were looking at Vikings' settlements, and again they found writings and etchings that looked like the letters of the Vikings of Norway. They saw the letters but have never been able to get enough scribbles or rune markings to make a sentence. To be truthful, I do not believe that an advanced race of aliens tried to make life difficult for us on earth by not leaving a distinct language behind. In fact, when one thinks about it, what language could they have left behind, as early humankind did not write or speak in full sentences when those aliens arrived?"

Alice said, "So you postulate aliens did the job of leaving behind remarkable buildings using the commonest stock around, which was stone? You believe that the precision of these buildings, which may include advanced measurements related to earth's demographics, might be a clue? You are also hinting that the order in the universe was also displayed as runes for future earthlings to advance their education of the cosmos when their time came in the future; is that it? I can accept that angle, and it is very clever, but much of this has been written by other novelists years ago."

She continued: "The writings may have been the afterthought of alien workers who remained on Earth when spoken language began to have order and to evolve. Maybe a few of these aliens settled down with their Earth families and remained until their deaths? They might have continued leaving clues in line with their professions or their tasks on the ship. If their ship left them, what else was there for them to do?"

# CHAPTER 21

# A Commander's Directive (Taken from an Old Manuscript in a Metal-Covered Binder: "Man, a Wandering, Searching Species")

After studying the manuscript again, Les interpreted: "Strange for our species and its evolution that our past is being uncovered by modern-day archaeologists. We have evolved from a race that built and lived in villages that grew into massive modern cities with all the amenities that any civilization could ever want or need. Our affluent societies have provided clean water and have recycled sewage, preventing our lakes, rivers and oceans from becoming overwhelmed with pollution. Many oceanic life forms that were nearing extinction have made a recovery to some extent. Wealth has given us a chance to repair the damage we have done to the environment and has caused the better use of all our resources through reduce, reuse and recycle."

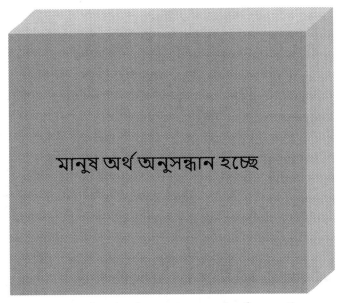

মানুষ অর্থ অনুসন্ধান হচ্ছে

Humankind: a being in search of meaning

Les's thoughts raced through an overworked brain as he again pondered to himself: *Yes, education of the masses and our scientists has made it possible to head to other planets. Using robotics, machines with artificial intelligence have landed on those planets in our solar system. All this was in preparation, to make it possible for human beings to physically visit them. Humankind's purpose is to see whether human life can exist and live there outside of Earth's atmosphere. Amongst the many reasons for humans to embark on such a risky undertaking is primarily to search for physical resources, which are near depletion on Earth and secondarily to continue to search the greatest frontier that is the cosmos.*

Les said to his wife, "You know, Love, too much spare time without direction does lead to boredom and can be the cause of self-destruction. The worst part is that such individuals tend to take all that is good in nature for granted."

Alice replied, "What is your point? All you have said is known fact!"

Les said, "When one gets everything one needs from society, it kills initiative and drive to advance society. A human being does not develop strength of character or courage when he has everything he needs. It certainly does not come from being happy all the time. It is only by surviving difficult times and challenging adversity that humankind grows and evolves into a better being."

Alice responded, "Aha! You believe that by humankind entering the cosmos, we will face all these challenges and become more evolved human beings. Maybe you are correct, but with the intense training and knowledge to run these spaceships, and being capable of withstanding all the terrors the cosmos could throw at them, surely these men and women are better beings than those of us who remain behind."

Les countered, "Sure. Should these men and women decide to mate and have children on another planet, the outcome for the infant could be a different being, even with the first pregnancy. But will the offspring of the next generation produce a different type of, a 'better,' human being? Could the environment have a dynamic impact on physiology and mental acuity so as to produce a different human?"

Alice said, "Wow! I can see where you are coming from, but surely the question cannot be absolute. There might be physiological changes as well as anatomical differences due to diet, gravity and a host of other influences. I mean, even radiation of various types, many of which we have no knowledge, could pass through protective clothing and make changes to the ova and sperm cells."

Les said, "Of course all that you have said is true, but the question remains: will there be after each generation an evolving, different human being?"

Alice answered, "Truthfully, my opinion? Yes, there may be changes that cause the extraterrestrial human beings to look different, maybe with a spare nose or with ten fingers on each hand, but essentially they will be human beings at their core."

Les said, "Satirical humour aside, their humanity will show through. Is that what you believe?"

Alice responded, "Yes."

Les said to her, "Strange you should believe as much. I must ask, which part of our physiological, psychological, anatomical or spiritual aspect will remain permanent and unchanging?"

Silence followed as they both knew that there was no answer, even if it was just a hypothetical/rhetorical question. The aged couple remained in their introspective moods, each looking at what was in front of them but seeing nothing. Their eyes remained unmoving, just staring at one undefinable spot, while their brains searched their neurological archives aimlessly.

These two scientists had spent most of their lives dealing with the hard sciences, and now, retired from their labs, their brain activity never seemed to rest. They decided to read whatever literature they enjoyed for that was one of the little things they thought retirees should do. They took to improving their garden, he designing it and her deciding on the types of plants and flowers that would fit against a huge cedar hedge. They supplemented each other's practical needs without knowing it. There were skirmishes when it came to execution of the plan, but everything was enjoyable in the end.

## Of Thoughts and Philosophy

Author Les, sipping his cold tea, said to Alice, "From all our historical searches on a few clever individuals who have excelled at the written word, what have we personally extracted for ourselves? I mean nothing to do with this project, Dear."

Alice said, "Strange you should ask such a question, because I was just thinking, why we enjoy this unsolvable predicament? After all, there is no reward, financial or otherwise, for the hours that we spend searching for answers."

Les interrupted her, saying, "That is easy. We were posed with a puzzle, and humans do not like puzzles. We, like most humans, embarked with great enthusiasm and a driving lust to find the answers."

Alice said, "A greater question entered my mind, and that is, why do I want to know? Why did the great ancient history that led to profound human philosophy, including the contradictory philosophies, become the basis of the great religions, the example being Hinduism, which began from a poem? Christianity began with historical accounts of a good man who claimed to be the Son of the one true God that were written four times by four of his followers in verse. Finally, the Islamic faith by way of the Koran was written by a man who hung around caravans listening to stories from Christians and Jews who already had the Torah."

Les asked, "What is the puzzle?"

Alice answered, "Well, these are all stories and I believe that many people were not educated and that negative thoughts and satire did not exist. I accept that the public at that time were gullible and had simplicity of thought; thus they learnt from highly emotionally charged stories and parables. These were taken from daily living occurrences. Why have such written stories remained in our modern educated times, allowing for billions to follow these religions with loyal intensity?"

"Go on!" Les said. "You seem to have a combined set of observances to complete not just the religious angles but also something more."

His wife smiling, said, "How perceptive of you, my dear! But really, many of these new philosophers and storytellers wrote their thoughts in verse. Why?"

Les said, "You have the atmosphere of this discussion; is there a particular author you could use as an example?"

Alice, scanning through the mass of reprints and a high stack of old books, some with pieces of paper marking a particular page or chapter, surrounding her, thought for a while, then quietly stated,

"Yes. In the translation of the poems by Lucretius, the author quotes from Epicurus when he was posed with the question of how we get our knowledge."

Les queried, "What was the response?"

Alice, looking at her handwritten notes, read out loud: "We get it through our senses and sensation. It is the only source of truth. It is the only reliable source of knowledge and consequently the only source of truth."

"A sensible answer, but it does not describe with examples, does it?"

"That is the problem," Alice replied. "He goes into a great diatribe on the different philosophies and every phenomenon then concludes that 'sensation gives direct evidence,' and in this case evidence is truth."

Les said, "I can accept that as a treatise for discussion. You see, humankind was acting as one organism unknown to itself like a flock of starlings that swerve around without crashing into each other."

"You what? What is it with you men that you can turn out these rash statements and then make deductions?" Alice asked.

"Excuse me, what do you mean by 'you men'?" Les questioned. "You asked, and maybe we feel that we must have an answer. While we do not understand why, we must provide an answer. This discussion misleads the focus of your question."

Alice calmed herself. "The logic of direct evidence and truth does ring true. If sensation does not give, or is unable to give, evidence because of its limitations, one is forced to accept theories that do not contradict the evidence that only our senses can interpret knowledge." She continued as if reading from her handwritten notes: "But the philosopher may arrive at more than one explanation for a given phenomenon. Even when there are several explanations that could be mutually exclusive or contradictory, they must all be accepted as being true."

Les smiled. "One of these explanations must be true in our world somewhere. Is that not true?"

"You bastard! You remember these arguments, do you not?"

"Not all of them, but I remember reading that work several times to try to understand where his logic was going, because what was rational to his mind in this world may be irrational in another world."

Alice countered, "You remember a lot more of the in-depth thought. He deduced that while one explanation may find a place in this world, the others will find their application in some other world out in the endless reaches of the infinitely varied universe."

"He covered himself nicely as our senses can give false information such as when we misjudge the size or colour of an object."

Alice said, "He explained that this was not the fault of the senses but, rather, that the data transmitted to the mind is incorrect. It is the mind that is in error for it misjudges the information correctly."

Les said, "Of course, our senses show us a material world that may portend a sole reality and why not, seeing all that surrounds us is material."

# CHAPTER 22

# Unusual Beings Dropping from the Star-Filled Heavens

The author hummed happily to himself as he sat alone. "Yes, it was in that dark period when an emancipation of earth's earlier tribes began. I believe this was when disparate groups of wandering primitives settled down because they were led to do so by powerful shamans or warlike leaders."

He paused then continued speaking to himself: "I wonder how much poetic 'scoundraling' I would be allowed here?"

"Whatever caused these tribes such as the Mayans, who were discovered in the modern country called Costa Rica (the Golden Coast)," he noted, "it was revealed that a civilization had settled down to a rich culture living in massive stone dwellings. Paved roads have been recently uncovered by modern-day archaeologists that reveal there are indicators of advanced tribes on the South American

144

continent. The whole concept of building these dwellings, implied by our archaeologists I believe, was to round out the story of these people. Ever the cynic, I believe this was done for the edification of the modern world, so that would find it easier to digest these hypothetical facts."

With cynicism he said, "It has the makings of a great story. At the same time there is the opportunity to increase income through grants for themselves and their research.

"Upheavals have been implied, namely that after a thousand years of building massive settlements, the Mayans formed trade routes between their northern neighbours and themselves. It was more a bartering system, exchanging grains such as corn and wheat for fish and other foods from the seaside natives. These supplies were paid to the Mayans in jadeite. This was a green precious stone that could be etched and carved with the faces and adornments of the leaders of the time. The Mayans, however, had large amounts of gold that were easily available from superficial mines and taken from their great rivers."

The old author sat back into his comfortable armchair in front of his computer and looked mindlessly through the window of his office.

"My problem," he said, yawning, "is, who was it that first suggested that this metal had a useful purpose? After all, the metal had been around them for many years. What happened to make them suddenly see the value of mining this metal and learning the whole process of gold smelting?

"Currently the whole idea of art in primitive peoples is appreciated by the wealthy, educated elite living in highly civilized communities, mainly in the northern cities of the planet. I know that I am lacking in this field of endeavour and that this implies a grain of geriatric dementia. So getting that out of the way, even I can see the beauty of these early creations in gold found in a modern-day Costa Rican museum, maybe because my grandfather and his son, my uncle, were goldsmiths from the nineteen twenties and thirties and I had seen their work as a child."

Les recalled: "My mother explained how clever her father, my grandfather, was at his trade. Her anecdotes explained how the family's wealth on her side of the family was obtained. She told us stories of wealthy East Indian families from the agrarian country districts who travelled long distances by horse in the early part of the twentieth century. From across the small island, they came to her father's shop in the capital. Only Grandfather could design and create specific jewellery for their families.

"I also saw the collection of work that my mother had, but she rarely wore any of those jewellery pieces in public. Unfortunately, these massive pieces of work were stolen by a family member in need. So it is not without some experience that I show appreciation for the goldsmith work done by the Mayans. Who taught them to work gold with such precision? Where were their equipment and forges? Where are the historic pieces from which they copied the designs?"

Mumbling to himself, he said, "So many unanswered questions. However, we are told that archaeologists uncovered evidence that these early peoples had an empire that covered much of South America. Their leaders adorned themselves in massive pieces of gold jewellery becoming of their status."

The old man muttered to himself as he reviewed the pieces of translation that his wife had printed out. He picked up a sheet from one of the documents and began to write:

> There was a revolution as leaders battled each other from neighbouring cities. It was deduced these battles did not entail the Mayan peoples, only the leaders and their upper-class followers. In fact, it was mainly a battle of the leaders in each city. There was little thought, should they kill each other off, to what would

happen to the rank-and-file population whom they were entrusted to lead.

"You know that bothers me!" he spoke aloud as his wife entered the office with bowls of soup.

She laid them on the desk, pushing away the printed papers, and asked, "What bothers you? What does not fit your manuscript?

"Come on!" she coaxed. "Lunchtime. I will bring in the cheese sandwiches with fresh Branson pickle on crusty Italian bread."

Almost immediately the old man seemed to come awake. "Ah, lunch! Soup and a cheese sandwich. I'll wash my hands and be right back." And with that he left the office.

## Lunch Break

The couple sat down and slurped their hot soup—the author's favourite, cream of broccoli—and of course enjoyed a buttered slice of crusty Italian ciabatta with it. They smiled and ate ravenously. Unusual for an aged couple, they still enjoyed eating heartily. Next to their plates were mugs of hot coffee they had begun to have every afternoon. For many years after their retirement, they thought having coffee after lunch prevented them from a good night's sleep. Without the coffee, however, they found they were beginning to enjoy an afternoon nap. Now having coffee at lunch, they remained awake. Napping in the afternoon had had to stop because research into the artifacts had become a bit of an obsession. They found they could sleep better at night because they were tired after all the reading and writing in the afternoons. They also agreed to eat later and set an active work schedule to solve the puzzle of these ancient artifacts. However, in doing so they both became enamored with reading, reviewing, searching and interpreting of the literary material they had uncovered. Of greater importance was that they were talking to each other as equals, and that seemed to have given a boost to their partnership.

Soup finished, mouths wiped with lots of serviettes, coffee in hand, they sat back. "Now tell me, what you have found out?" Alice asked Les.

He looked up after quietly sipping the hot black bitter liquid to which he had become addicted.

"It appears that a leadership had evolved amongst an elite of chosen individuals in the early evolution of humankind. Paying attention to a leader came as a result of settling down from a migratory lifestyle. My problem is, who chose the leaders and placed them into leadership positions? The leaders seem to have garnered knowledge as to the times of the year when it was best to sow crops. They also appeared to know when it was propitious to reap and what to do when agriculture efforts failed. With such knowledge, the crops were successful and the workers were told to store away a portion of the grain. In the off planting season, lots of grain was distributed, so the workers ate healthily from stores of grain."

Les continued, "This sort of advanced planning and execution using all-important food storage must have required discussion and planning abilities. When there was a shortfall as a result of poor harvest for one of a number of reasons, leaders instructed the masses on how to cope. Of course the leaders led, but they took advantage of their position to serve themselves first (as a comedian once said, 'It is good to be king'). Supposedly the masses also understood the leaders came first.

"Well, who made the leaders and gave them the knowledge of agriculture, water storage and engineering of the streams to better serve the masses? Similarly, someone had to teach primitives the technology of road building so they could move goods and massive rocks more easily for building within the city."

He stood up, cup of coffee in hand. "Oh! I could see it all unfolding, and it seemed to be normal in an evolving society. Why did they not teach the people to do these tasks on their own? Maybe leaders kept the seeds to replant the following season, depriving workers of their independence in not having their own seeds to plant, thus maintaining control. But nowhere has there been any archaeological evidence of attempts by the rank and file to take over and topple the leadership or of the usurping of storage bins of harvested grain. So the leadership, however chosen, had complete control of the workers." He turned away from the window.

"Absolute power corrupts absolutely. Was that the cause?" Alice asked.

Les's up until now quiet spouse continued, "That would imply a two-tiered group of people, one with all the knowledge to lead and to organize manpower to build and maintain a civilization. Only a few picked by bribery and largesse would become the selected individuals related to the leaders, leaving the masses in an unevolved state, in fact, primitive."

"Exactly. You have nailed that down. How can one expect such a restrictive vision capable of building a civilization? Good leadership in those times meant keeping power over others because of their knowledge and using force. A chief would keep a son or daughter to take over when he died. He would have a plan of secession, and there was none, at least at this stage. Surely a good soldier would see this as an opportunity to take power. There must have been great fighters/warriors even if they came from chosen hangers-on. But holding power by force brings down thinking and planning only to keep power. Where are the far-thinking planners and organizers?"

Alice, the shrewd mate, asked, "You have a plan, haven't you?"

Les smiled. "I shall tell you as I write it down quickly for fear of losing the train of thought.

"Any leadership blessed by a superior being will have a limited shelf life because such a leader will have gotten the position without working or striving for the privilege.

"Such has been the history throughout the emergence of humankind into *Homo sapiens*, whatever that means," the author continued.

"I believe in the absence of evidence. It is my hypothesis or, say, rather a postulate that such puppets were placed with limited knowledge on what true leadership entails. They were given just enough information for the survival of the clan or tribe by providing a food source that was constant. This did not demand any thinking on their part. Having seen the work of powerful individuals or beings who constructed the pyramids and roads, they copied the same end intent from what they had observed." He stopped.

Les then continued, "There is modern-day evidence to support this concept that some workers may have assisted the powerful aliens in what they were constructing without recognizing the technology used."

His wife looked on passively. This was the part she loved to see when it came to displaying his infectious imagination.

Les was on a roll: "These powerful aliens remained as long as was needed to complete instructions for Earth's primitive primates, recently turned into upright humans. The basic stuff for enhancing a cognizant being was already available, and with basic genetic interference or engineering, a worthwhile being would evolve. On planet Earth, it was the aliens' mission to lead by example. In doing so, they focused on what earthlings should contemplate apart from the dietary requirements to survive: namely, they should understand the role of their star.

"It was the aliens' idea to make life simple using the Sun as a celestial clock that portrays all that Earth's life forms require to live on this planet."

The old author was in free fall as his mind conjured up different possibilities. Not letting facts get in his way, he stared enigmatically at the computer screen.

"It was a good choice for a simple primate life form with a capacity to learn. In fact it was what primitive life forms required for survival. I hypothesize that powerful aliens went around the planet using the commonest of all available stock on the planet, large rocks, and they moved them to lay out an explanation of how Earth exists in the solar system. To construct pointers to the Sun, it was necessary to tie that knowledge to food production, a necessity to the primates' survival.

"Appealing to the primates' sense of wonder, the aliens, at the end of the day, went back to their orbiting ship, circulating the Sun between two planets, of which Venus shone the brightest while Mercury just had a presence. This was the little knowledge, I hypothesize, that was revealed to their chosen leaders.

"The aliens treated different primitives around planet Earth the same way. It was necessary to give the same message, but using different pointers. I suggest that alien teams went around the planet and repeated the act of construction using massive stones cut out of mountainsides. Using antigravity strips, they lifted and moved the massive stones and placed them accurately one on top of the other or organized them into a circle that was in accordance with the different seasons."

The aged author paused then continued as his gnarled fingers covered the keyboard. "They did these tasks openly because they wanted the primitives to duplicate this type of work. The pointers or educational markers were left around the planet for communities to learn and, if possible, imitate. By living together, much more could be achieved, especially when they worked on a defined project. Food could be sown in fields using nearby water reserves, so the need for groups to remain nomadic vanished. By remaining in groups, there was extra time freed up, so earthlings began to define and streamline their surroundings.

"While the historic timing may be inaccurate for my postulate, it is pretty much within a similar timeline. Similarly, deductions have been uncovered in the construction of the pyramids in Egypt, South America and Thailand, as well as erecting giant rock circles at Stonehenge in England where many more, have since been uncovered.

"Mind you, if there were superior beings that came with a plan to develop life on Earth and did all that I have ventured to suggest, there was great thought in not having one tribe own more than another. It would have brought about antagonism between those with the most and those who were less fortunate.

"It seems that while the Mayans may have mastered all aspects of mining rocks, carving them out from the sides of mountains and rivers, they were not as resourceful in handling the streams and water pools. They may have copied the sanding effect of erosion that produces the round smooth river boulders. In doing so, they mastered the art of making massive stone balls, in fact of different sizes, that could be rolled on the packed stone roads now being uncovered in South America."

After a thoughtful pause, Les continued: "One can presuppose that these smooth round stones were copied after observing the shape of the planets from atop the pyramids. The stones appear to look like the planets in our solar system. This would make sense since the aliens had taught them all these wonderful things pointing to the sun. Of course, this fact was unknown to the native populace. As an earthbound population, they would assume godlike forms went back to their home in the sky or heavens.

"You see, Love, on the other hand the Aztecs knew how to bring water into safe canals, which were used as a transport system. The water was also safe for drinking and for watering the floating gardens that grew fruits on small trees, along with tomatoes, carrots, potatoes and a variety of edible vegetables. This is what they had to trade with the Mayans, and jade stones were desired by the Mayan leaders. Mayan leaders used gold as decoration, placed around their necks and bodies, and as a form of payment."

A strong voice interrupted, "Slow down, Love. You are moving too far away from the first important point. Why not use the deductions of modern-day anthropologists and their counterparts, the archaeologists who have made significant discoveries? Even though there may be a bit too much supposition in the conclusions made more for academic convenience and thesis. What do you think?"

"Bloody brilliant, if I may say so. Do we have the printouts?" Les anxiously moved towards his computer again.

Reviewing the documents, he went silent. After about twenty minutes he looked up and saw his wife holding up a page to him, which he silently took and began to read.

He began, "In light of modern-day archaeological findings, the authors produced these facts. The leadership was killed off through their wars with neighbouring tribes. The remaining peoples disappeared into the forests, where many died of starvation. Only a few still remain today. There were records made as the Mayans knew how to document their work. All they had accomplished was documented and placed into books.

"I do not know how this statement came about, but it states that over one thousand books were destroyed, which seems a bit outlandish to me, but it is in a scientific journal," he muttered.

"It is presumed that these books were kept by a chosen few quiet, gentle individuals. How did they learn to write? Why did they write down their history and culture? How did this society end? What were the materials used to make books? We understand papyrus paper, but what did the Mayans use?

"Apparently four books were found with an estimated date of August 13, 300 BC, quite specific. However, these books deal more with astronomy, which was a major focus at the time. It has been suggested that the Mayans focused on the planet Venus, but no reason has been given for this hypothesis to date. The other books reveal advanced mathematics predating Galileo."

Thoughtfully, he spoke quietly to his now silent wife, "Maybe the scribes of this history were the old ones left behind by the visiting aliens. The scribes were told to document all that had happened with the primates' evolution as they were old and did not wish to continue in a metallic ship coursing through the dark cosmos. It would be the ideal way to end such a life as an alien retiree with a purpose. How is that for conjecture, eh?"

Alice laughed. "You are a writer of fiction and no better than the enthusiastic archaeologists with their presumptions."

# CHAPTER 23

# Physical Characteristics of the Alien

## Abstraction

Mumbling as he did so, Les the author wrote the following:

> The extraterrestrial beings were large, almost eight
> feet tall, and their heads were big, almost square.
> The size of the head could be misconstrued by
> the primitives as the aliens may have used helmets
> that had optimal air mixture. The drawings on the
> lithographs found in caves do not show details. The
> primitive cave dwellers drew what they thought they
> saw and left cave etchings lacking detail or insight.
> Their benefactors were dressed in different types of
> armour and carried strange tools with them.

They used a light we now know as a laser to cut stones, then added antigravity strips, which allowed the heaviest and largest stones to be easily lifted and taken to a building site already prepared by a few of these giants. Two used flame-throwers and fire to clear the site and to level the ground. After the aliens flattened the site and pounded stones around it to form a massive clear area, called a plaza, they proceeded to build the pyramid.

Roads were built making use of flat stones that created a hard path free of brambles and tree clutter. It was thought that these roads were used to assist in the movement of giant rocks brought from as far away as ten miles or more to the building site. They had to be lifted and transported to the site, where a pyramid was erected on the prepared area.

Les paused and bent his head to his chest as if having a nap.

## Interruption

A whisper came from the aged book: "At the top of the pyramid, the powerful leader lived, an officer of Sig from Commander Sitla's ship. That ship had taken an orbit and was circling the sun. From where he sat at the apex of the pyramid, he could monitor his ship's orbit.

"In the pyramid, rooms below housed officers and those professionals responsible for the physical construction, while others directed the working crew on the site. Food was planted in rows of crops in the fields outside the city walls. The grains produced were used by the aliens, who used shuttles to move between their ship and the planet. The natives looked on at all the activity from the cover of the forests and bushes. The aliens gave these natives a taste of the food made from the surrounding plants.

"Slowly the bands of primitives began to help the aliens, who organized the primitives to assist in building the pyramids. The aliens returned to their ship daily, and the natives saw them as Gods in the sky. It became ritual for them to look up and ask that the God return to feed them and teach them when daylight returned.

"By this time the aliens began to include primitives as workers who performed simple tasks, and slowly the concept of organized labour began to take shape. The primitive Mayans had work and were paid with gifts of food that they enjoyed. This benefit was extended by having assistance in building their own round houses to keep their families safe. The family was employed in agriculture by attending to the sowing of seeds, watering them and cleaning the community village, and later on in reaping the crops."

## Humanity

Without friends, no one would choose to live, even though he had all the other goods.

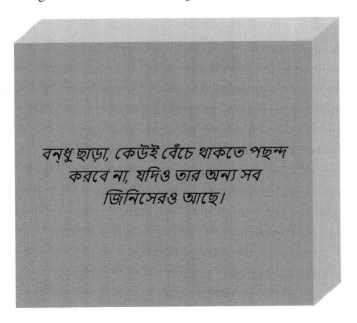

# Research Continued

Of cues and clues with hints and pointers: intelligent alien life forms from our past.

Les, alone, spoke out loud: "There is a giant drawing arranged in stones on the side of the Andes mountains depicting a large arrow pointing to the peak of the mountain. When followed, as is directed, to the top of the mountain, there is a flattened plaza. It is marked off by stones arranged as a defined clear area. At each corner there are enormous geoglyphs, one depicting a hummingbird in great detail, while other animals are similarly defined on the other three corners. These were creatures common to that part of earth's forested biome.

"Now referred to as the Nazca lines, these drawings are estimated to have come into existence around AD 1–700. The largest geoglyphs are calculated to be approximately twelve hundred feet in length. This marked quadrant can be seen clearly only from the air using modern aviation. It is not unfair for modern anthropologists to deduce that it was made for aeronautical landing crafts.

"If that is not the explanation, then one has to ask, what else was the purpose of these well-marked areas that can be seen from outer space? Why build these stone glyphs that can only be seen from above?" muttered the author, looking at the mystical antique materials that had landed in his hands.

He surmised under his breath as he typed his manuscript.

An Alien Perspective

Thousands of workers from the ship came and went in landing parties on different parts of planet Earth. Their one mission was to repeat the same tasks: build pyramids to suit the area using rocks mined from a distant location, or so it appeared to be to one group of native onlookers. Let the natives look on at what is being done, give them food and water, allow them to watch and keep them nearby for as long as possible.

The purpose was to encourage the natives to join in the building process without giving away any of the technology used. The simplest way was to entrap them with food. Prepared foods from surrounding crops like wheat, barley, corn, peas, beans and root vegetables (yams, potatoes, eddoes, cassava, etc.) were all available and close at hand. To support this belief, consider the Akshardham Temple, a massive structure 370 ft. long by 317 ft. wide with carvings of flora and fauna as well as of usual musicians and dancers. It is the plants and other botanical species that are inscribed.

Further evidence one brings to support this hypothesis is the ancient Voynich Manuscript written in a language that no scholars to date have been able to decipher, another failure of archaeologists. This is a 700-year-old manuscript that depicts plants and herbs, none of which are known to exist on Earth, but the aliens used these botanical plants native to their planet, Sig. Maybe this manuscript is a hoax, but to what end? Was human sense of humour developed at that stage of history?

Alien intentions were to allow curiosity in these primates to cause them to look at what was being done by these visitors to their planet. The aliens believed that the primitives would one day emulate their work and copy their buildings. At the same time, it was necessary for Earth's primates to witness foods being planted by the aliens. Encourage them to do the same and let them reap their own food; show them how to use fire to prepare and boil these easily obtained roots, greens, seeds and vegetables without hunting.

Success came when the earthlings began to make buildings for themselves. Finally, earthling primitives were encouraged to build homes of stone. Currently these natives were building shacks from fallen branches to cover their roofs to keep the rain away. The aliens showed them they could build their homes high off the ground to protect them from floods that threatened to destroy their homes or kept them from having to sleep on the wet ground.

Les, mumbling to himself, said, "Another benefit of building homes on posts higher up was protection from the onslaught of insects that attacked them while they slept on the ground. It would also prevent fleas and lice from infecting their skin and hair. This type of leadership by example could best be seen in the construction of the Sacsayhuaman Walls built around AD 1400 by over twenty thousand workers. This ruin still survives as a marvel of wonder for there is no single binding agent keeping the massive stones together.

"The population came together, and this encouraged crossbreeding as mixed genes allowed for healthier hybrids. Remaining in one group, village or township for long periods of time, the primitives' common needs were met as a collective. This allowed native groups to build, after seeing what the aliens had done, temples such as Tikal and, later on, Baalbek Heliopolis, where the Greeks, it was thought, showed others how to build. There was a building in Lebanon with fifty-four columns, the Temple of Jupiter. Next to the Temple of Bacchus were more, maybe up to six temples.

"However, the more mundane needs of such a group included clean water supply and walls around the village to keep away carnivores such as jaguars and bears and enemies from other villages. To satisfy the gods that showed them all the good things they were enjoying, the primitives erected the temples of Saint Sava and Christ the Saviour.

"However, such bands of early humans left an archaeological trail of broken homes and earthenware. This gave the archaeologists a road map of how primitive races lived on Earth. It was an unwritten history of early humankind evolving into the race we are today."

# CHAPTER 24

# Circles of Great Standing Rocks—Why?

## A Dissertation

The aged author reviewed the large pile of printed literature that his scientific-trained wife had downloaded and printed after reviewing his requests. He summed up his thoughts then read aloud in his cluttered home office. His spouse had gone grocery shopping.

"The Greek historian Herodotus was one of the first archaeologists in history and was referred to as the 'Father of History.' A lot of time has passed since the fifth century BC, when Herodotus inspired archaeologists to branch out and search for lost artifacts relating to human existence. Yes, dig it up! Find our past history and examine how we got to this scholarly present."

"Mmm! That seemed like a good way to begin. And why not?

What was the right way to start trying to solve this puzzle of erected rocks in a circle? What was its purpose?

"Circles made on the surface of the ground from rounded boulders to represent the planets in the heavens above were laid out for early communities of people to observe and maybe learn from. Instead of learning, though, many of our predecessors, primitive tribes of peoples, looked for symbolism to which to attribute their good fortunes. These simple folks saw who brought them the largesse. It must have been gods that gave them regular food and showed them how to provide for themselves."

The author then spoke to his wife, who had returned from her grocery shopping: "You know the indicators have all been found. I do not wish to go into the Stonehenge phenomenon. I must, however, admit I am disappointed with the UK scholars of the day who have let the first suggested opinions be the only answer. Quite honestly, to me it was a snap opinion for academic convenience. They have expended very little energy trying to solve the puzzle, nay, the enigma that it is. Now there is all this commercial crap about Druids and magic."

"What exactly did you expect from them?" Alice quietly asked. Before Les could respond, she said, having sat down and now looking at her screen, "You know that both anthropology and archaeology are not concrete sciences in the strictest sense. These disciplines are both based on supposition, hypothesis and conjecture."

"Exactly," replied the author, looking up at the ceiling contemplatively. "You have hit it on the head. I mean, all these chaps with university grants are still little boys going on an adventure for the weekend. They leave home, taking their sandwiches from their mums, saying, 'I will see you later, Mum.' Only in their case, university grants are being expended to watch them chip away at flint stones to reveal tools that can cut meat or spear tips that can puncture hide.

"I will bet you there are more of these stone tools made by modern anthropologists lying in old museum boxes than made by the cavemen they were trying to understand. Oh! By the way, I got thrown out of the anthropology classes at Waterloo after I was caught giggling. My science partner laughed out loud when we were shown a whole skull made of white plastic material that was delicately taken from a brown lacquered box.

"The professor solemnly placed the skull on the table in front of the auditorium. My friend whispered to me under his breath, 'Gops, all that was made from a single tooth.' The professor promptly called us out and asked us to leave the auditorium. I was ashamed at the time, but I could not stop laughing at the silliness of showing the skull bones that were 80 per cent plastic. It was the lecturer's overwhelming enthusiasm that became silly. On the other hand, I may have missed out on learning whether the defining piece revealed human beings lived in Olduvai. So what?"

Alice said, "We must not be too hard on them. In the case of Stonehenge, they have actually calculated the date to be around 3000 to 2000 BC. Furthermore, they are able to show that the alignment of the stones coincides with the winter and summer solstices. That should be worth something to you, eh?"

Les said, "That is exactly what I mean. There is a positive proven fact to enlighten the people of the day. The ancient Brits were still painted blue. They had no idea what a solstice was, did they? They did not have a clue as to when to plant their crops because it was still trial and error by remarkable primitive humans undergoing evolution. There was no intelligence or skilled leadership to move such massive designed stones just for a function. My goodness! They still believed in mystical powers from the swamplands that surrounded them.

"Witches and spirits had inside knowledge of the future and could bring about the future using mystery while granting wishes. Today the concept brings great comic relief. Indeed, I believe a comedian referred to these tales as coming from 'watery tarts.'"

Alice, still looking at her screen absent-mindedly, stated, "Do not become academically agitated with these findings to date, Dear. After all, only you and I are working on these mysteries because you were selected to do so. Look at how much we are learning and refreshing our memories. What else would you rather be doing, eh?"

Les replied, "Goodness. How lucky can I be to have such a clever woman by my side, willing to have us take a reality check? That is truly useful to bring me down to earth when I wander off into righteous indignation and academic self-analysis. Oh yes, and also to correct all my failings in the cold light of female dispassionate logic!"

Alice countered, "That is also called loyalty and love, if you would take time to think of my input. What else could I be doing in retirement, more crosswords, reading the BBC news from around the world? In fact, throughout our, quote, retirement years, you have provided more income and have gotten yourself hooked on a hobby where I could have been left out. Your enthusiasm and obvious love for novel writing is a thing of great envy. I love you for including me in the reading and the plot of your books. I will get our tea. And I have a surprise for your palate: English tarts."

The author, smiling above his wrinkled, sagging chin, said, "Be still, my thumping heart. A tart at my age could be destructive, you know. Anyway, I have you, so bring it on!"

Looking through his notes, he fell into deep concentration. "The proof surely is the number of broken-down circles, which would suggest bad copying by the early natives.

"The same could be said of the universal false stone structures that did not withstand the passage of time. Objects of primitive copying by simpler minds that were found deteriorated close to the original, wonderful structures that withstood time, remaining well into the twenty-first century. That has to be the partial answer as found in parts of Africa, where modern African travellers record broken-down sand pyramids They have tried to portray to the world that there was a golden age of an African empire."

Les spoke under his breath, "In fact, these structures were bad copies of the real stone pyramids from Egypt, and these primitives tried to duplicate them without any lasting effect."

His thoughts flowed: "The aliens revealed true brilliance by building under the oceans a pyramid, and just maybe a few aliens remained on Earth not connected to the major project. Near his end, an alien would have explained the mystery of the city of Atlantis that has circulated in myths and legends. However, long lines of cut oblong stones have been uncovered under the Atlantic Ocean outlining a pathway, but again the archaeologists stopped."

Les exclaimed, "My goodness, no one took the time to make a comparison as this was no different from the Nazca pathway landing sites. Not one scientific mind followed up, asking where these well-organized stone edges had been mined or, what's more, how these giant carved stones were moved from land to a defined path. Where did they lead to? Hypothesis would suggest that deep beneath the oceans there could have been a whole city. Modern-day scholars are satisfied, for purposes of expediency, to drop into speculation and hypotheses, which are more palatable to the public.

"Suggesting that it must have been an old wall of a shoreline community that had been washed away by sea storms or a tsunamis of the past, mmm! Very convenient indeed!

"However, look at the moai faces on Easter Island. Some academic chap, maybe an anthropologist, I believe, went over there to try to determine how the large stone faces could be moved. OK, he had the sculptures that were cut a long distance from the sea edge. He attempted to use his university students to experiment on how they were dragged to the edge of the seashore to face across the ocean."

Alice asked, "How did that work out?"

Les answered, "Not too bad, actually. After many attempts at dragging these huge masses of heavy stones on logs, which the natives had supposedly cut down the forests to make rollers, he found out it could not be done as the process of lying the stone mass on its back shattered the stone image and the rollers. Add to this the need for literally hundreds of people to pull the stone carving. It was not practical, plus the island did not have a large enough population to cut the effigy then transport it.

"However, when the anthropologist's team stood the face up on its footing, it could be danced by slowly moving it from right to left in little steps."

Alice said, "Well, that sounds like success, doesn't it?"

Les replied, "Maybe. This worked when moving the statues on level ground, but if you look at where the faces are mounted, they are on mounds that are quite high. One can envisage that they would become top-heavy on a slope and would fall backwards."

Alice remarked, "Well, even I could see the fault in that physical attempt."

Les put in, "You see, my predicament is with the researcher who just went ahead and said that what he did was possible because it worked with his team. The problem I have is that he did not complete the assignment, which was to drag the completed faces to elevated sites. He abandoned the experiment after moving or dancing his stone images on flat ground. He returned to the university quite pleased with himself and wrote a paper, after which he received more grant money to continue the same work. Oh! He would also lecture to large classes of naive students taking archaeology to get an easy credit."

Alice admonished, "Do not get bitter; it does not become you. Silly old man." She giggled.

Les said, "But you see what I mean. Do you know that on the backs of these moai heads there are etchings or runes? According to the literature, they are undecipherable. These etchings are quite well-defined and are now referred to as 'codes,' making the whole idea even more mysterious for a researcher such as myself."

Les continued speaking: "Supposing I was to use this knowledge as it now stands in the literature and suggest that maybe aliens might have landed there to study the natives. They wanted to leave a sign that a sentient life form was here, so they left the heads, as seen by the primitives in their current place, which was the direction from whence they came.

"The aliens would have used their stonecutting lasers and antigravity strips to move the heavy stones, which would take little to no effort. The natives saw them arrive in their shuttles from across the water. They wanted the aliens to return, and the best place was from whence they'd come. So the faces stood looking outwards."

Alice said, "Well, that is a great concept and good enough to be in your work of fiction. No one would dispute your imagination."

Les said to her, "Do not even start me off with the pyramids in Egypt and all that crap about slaves building the Great Pyramids. As a young man, I once heard a true breakdown of the pyramid statistics that could be used as a teaching tool based on detailed measurements of Earth's dimensions that were built into their architecture."

Alice, still focused on her tablet, spoke up, "Go on. You have my attention."

"From what I can remember—do not hold me to the actual figures—the average pyramid weighs over six million tons. At its peak, the tallest is four hundred and ninety feet tall. The startling thing is that it faces true north of the planet about three and six-tenths of a degree. There are some calculations using the height and multiplying by forty-three thousand two hundred, which is the measurement of the circumference of the earth. Some of the blocks of stone weigh in excess of seventy tons and were raised to a height upwards of three hundred feet.

"In old Egypt with the tools of the day, this would have been an impossibility. Apparently the earth wobbles every seventy-two years and the mathematics suggest that if one were to take forty-three thousand two hundred precision readings of a one-degree base, it would be the same as the circumference of earth. The truth of these facts reveals there was another accurate dimensional degree that explains the demographics of the earth."

After a pause, Les said, "You see, my dear, this was space age engineering, but of more importance is that it was built with an artistic precision. And what an achievement. No slave labour could produce such refinement in construction or engineering, not even with our present-day skills. Think of it! How could Stone Age humans know about these measurements?"

# CHAPTER 25

# The Artificial God Anointed Native Leaders (Author's Notes Taken from the Literature Search)

"In light of primitive peoples, from the literature of the anthropologists, we are led to believe that these wanderers were always on the move, searching for food. It is suggested that they followed herds of herbivores as they migrated across the great grass plains of the planet, following the weather changes of rain and dry weather."

Judge a man by his questions, not by his answers.

—Voltaire

## Role of Wealth in Human Development

Alice, wife of the venerable Les, said, "You know, Dear, you should handle the role of wealth in leadership. It is only with wealth that any society would have a reason to work. Wealth and the show of wealth reveals the benefits of fine living. This could stoke the primitive mind to want to obtain similar possessions. What do you think?"

Les replied, "Yes. I have placed a number of such notes in a stack on the desk somewhere here. I could show that wealth was an essential driving force in the development of early societies. This cube would suggest that early humankind was told by a supreme being, God, that if you copy the trimmings of a leader, you too could be wealthy. The antithesis of such a goal would not necessarily be true; however, good living requires wealth. Yes! I think I have a twist on this. In European history, the wealthy kings and princes built huge castles, palaces and churches in their names. Such industry gave employment to many, and trades were developed. Having a trade and regular work, the common man could have a home for his family as well as food."

Turning his attention elsewhere, Les said, "Now let us examine these historical documents of the aliens or godlike life forms that interfered on Earth. For instance, the metal aluminum was uncovered from the Chinese Jin dynasty in approximately AD 265–420, more than two thousand years ago. It was also discovered in Russia from a chunk of coal containing aluminum. Humankind was not around to manufacture that type of alloy, and the energy needed for these products to be formed would be impossible for a still evolving primate to harness. The only way that could have happened would be a flaming or molten debris/asteroid dropping onto earth and combining the ingredients to form aluminum.

"Let me see! Around that time, there was a similar occurrence. Yes! There were findings called the Roman dodecahedron headpiece in the shape of a diving mask from antiquity. It was thought to be made of bronze. Later anthropologists suggested that these were used by Roman sailors to find their geographic direction across the surrounding seas. Again a simplistic explanation/answer with no evidence to support these suggestions or hypotheses."

Muttering to himself, Les continued, "But there was another mining incident that produced unusual findings. Ah! Here it is, the chalk ovoids from approximately sixty-five million years ago that look 'man-made'—the archaeologist said it is from the Cretaceous Period. Humans were millions of years away from coming into existence. This must have been the work of an advanced society or an extraterrestrial entity, is my suggestion."

Alice said, "You know you are drifting away from your focus on alien intervention. Why not stick to the evidence of wealth in society?"

Les answered, "You are quite correct. What I wanted was the document on the Sanxingdui Treasures. Yes! A most unusual ancient, again Chinese, city named Sanxingdui. Today, it is referred to as

Sichuan. The archaeologists found jade relics covered with gold, and they appeared to have been buried well over three thousand years earlier."

Alice said, "When I hear you repeat these findings that you have placed into novel format, I ask myself, who made these treasures? Why did they make them? Obviously they were the work of a trained artist/artisan who made money/wealth for himself. He may have had to make these items to the specifications of a wealthy lord or leader. But the intricate work is that of a thinking artisan with an unusual skill." More questions derived from her literature search.

Les replied, "However, it is stated in our medieval manuscript the mention of the Scrolls of Qumran, which describe hidden treasure, none of which was ever found. Several opinions come to mind, that wealth was to be secured then based on its value and then be hidden away. Like the animals' behaviour on earth, human beings can obtain food or possessions by picking the fruit from a tree, or by furtively stealing, or by using force to take it away. Wealth is then transferred to another person either by force or cunning. Transfer of wealth meant transfer of power from one individual to another, more powerful individual." Les made these deductions based on what a primitive mind would conceive.

Alice said, "You know, this focus on the novel, namely that aliens may have been here either before humankind arrived on the scene or when early humankind was evolving, may have some merit. As you have uncovered and suggested, they left clues of their presence, and that in itself would have been enough to stimulate human beings to begin using their brains. If early human beings saw what others could do, they likely followed by imitating the aliens. Now modern human beings are investigating why these artifacts are here on earth, since early humankind was incapable of doing such sophisticated work. If there had not been another civilization or an advanced human civilization, these items would have been destroyed."

Thoughtfully she continued, "Similar to the dinosaurs' destruction after the meteorite slammed into earth, there had to be aliens living on or visiting this planet in those early days. Or is that too far a reach?"

Les said, "I do not suppose there is any chance of getting a hot cup of green tea, is there, Love?"

"Sure. It is time for a tea break as in a cricket match, eh?"

# CHAPTER 26

# Ancient Artifacts: What Do They Tell?

Les, sitting back on his old armchair, said, "I am close to the 'why' factor, you know, Dear! It does not seem complete, almost as if it is on the tip of my tongue. The answer remains elusive."

Thinking quietly, cup of hot tea in hand, he worked out in his mind, "First of all the aliens would have built structures all over the planet wherever there was a native population. This was necessary for all tribes of human beings to be exposed to a similar activity. Ancient temples built over the years were first shown as small drawings in caves or were started as projects that allowed for native workers to complete them. What better way for them to learn?

"Afterwards, there must have been, as there probably still are, many hybrids of these aliens around. While the majority would have died out and others would have left on the departing mother ship, it is possible that a number of alien workers remained behind, continuing the building projects begun by their founder. That leader, for unknown reasons, would have left this solar system in a new ship with a new crew. On the other hand with a massive crew, the many born in transit would have taken the opportunity to visit and land on a real planet. Maybe a number joined the work teams from the aliens' ship.

"The aliens built in Egypt and in South America as seen by the Mayan and Aztec peoples. A pyramid was found under the Sea of Galilee in Israel. It is massive with an estimated weight of over sixty thousand tons and a height of thirty-two feet. Yes, only a superior alien life form with superior knowledge of technological and engineering skills could have built such a monument on planet Earth. Our archaeologists suggest that it was first built on dry land and, with encroachment of the sea, sank below the waters—very convenient, eh!"

Mumbling, Les said, "Maybe I should highlight the other, less popular sites. Let me list these structures: Angkor Wat, twelfth century AD, with an outer gallery of six hundred and fourteen by seven hundred and five feet and a height of two hundred and thirteen feet. Next is Egypt's Karnak Hypostyle Hall of fifty thousand square feet with one hundred and thirty-four columns in sixteen rows, the highest column standing at eighty feet. This is quite a list that my wife has composed. Borobudur, a Buddhist temple in Indonesia on Java, was built sometime in the eighth or ninth century."

He continued speaking to himself: "The measurements are quite interesting to me but boring to the readers. Next, there is Akshardham Temple, decorated with flora and fauna of the region and great artwork—very detailed. Then we have Sri Ranganathaswamy, on one hundred and fifty-six acres of land and standing over two hundred feet tall. Such massive dimensions built by early humankind? I do not think so. Finally, I dare say there are a lot more, but I have mentioned enough to salve my novel intentions, such as Jetavanara Maya, built around the third century, four hundred feet tall, while the pyramids at Giza are four hundred and eighty feet."

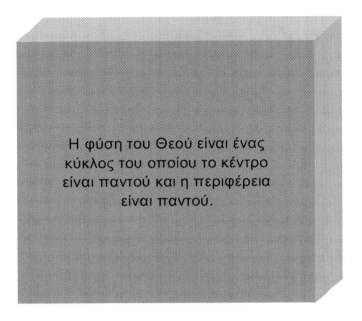

Η φύση του Θεού είναι ένας κύκλος του οποίου το κέντρο είναι παντού και η περιφέρεια είναι παντού.

The nature of God is a circle, of which the centre is nowhere and the circumference is everywhere.

*Empedocles*

Alice has suggested that Les describe The role of Gold and Jade figurines used in trade exchanges.

Les said, "Wealth played a major role in the past but also has affected latter-day explorers who have undertaken risky endeavours to find these treasures. For instance there are many maps that claim to show where wealth or treasure has been buried and hidden away. Rumour has it, and false maps have been found claiming, that certain maritime wealth was captured by pirates and hidden away in odd places. Rarely has any of this treasure been recovered, but there has been some success of recovered wealth by deep sea divers searching for pirate treasure that was being transported from South

America to Spain during the 1500s. Whereas wealth in a different era accumulated by the pharaohs was found in burial sites as in the pyramids of King Tut.

"Humankind rapidly evolved, and there appeared to be a need to please the Deity. Hence gold jewellery, precious stones and jade, which leaders coveted, was left to the Deity from their own collections. Humankind had to come to appease God or the Deity when death was close at hand. Simplification in thinking stimulated the religious belief that there was a way to get to their deity upon leaving Earth. The medieval thinking at that time felt was that there was a portal to God somewhere in the heavens looking upwards or into the solar system. Towards that end, the rank and file of humankind, the poor or less endowed who could not fly off or join God using boats, may have reasoned that perhaps there was a different way to reach paradise."

"They knew it would be physically tedious, but tedium was nothing new to the hard-working general masses. Such an archaeological site was found in Russia, named Bolshoi Zayatsky Island, where stone labyrinths supposedly leading to the underworld were discovered."

## Astrological Signs

Author Les muttered in his office, "Yes, there are many stone geographic markers that human beings have discovered, but true explanations are more difficult to fathom. While the human species are storytellers, fiction with hyperbole leaves explanations in the realm of hypothesis. On the other hand, there is the Piri Reis Map of 1513 showing Antarctica well before humankind knew of its existence—which humanity discovered three hundred years later."

"While divers were exploring deep sea wrecks, from one ship a most unusual piece of engineering referred to as the Antikythera mechanism was found. It has been dated at around two thousand years. It was called an astrological phenomenon, and that was the end of the story, with no one asking who had such technology or how old the shipwreck was. So much left without explanation!"

Les continued composing on his computer and enjoying the process as he strongly felt that these clues, these markers and other alien-made futuristic pieces of technology all combined to show that aliens were here long before humankind had totally evolved into a thinking primate. There was one other point that consistently revealed early humankind did not have what it took to produce the accuracy housed within these structures. Modern researchers have shown using modern-day mathematics and computers that the measurements these early beings made of planet Earth are accurate.

Using carbon dating, archaeologists have shown when these buildings were constructed. In those time periods, human beings did not know the Earth was round and revolved around the Sun. However, built into these structures was this fundamental knowledge about planet Earth long before modern humankind had emerged.

Les wrote, "The three pyramids—Khufu (Cheops), Khafre (Chephren) and Menkaure (Mycerimus)—were built between 2700 and 2500 BC as royal tombs. The largest and most impressive of these pyramids is Khufu, which covers thirteen acres and is believed to be made of more than two million stone blocks that weigh from two to thirty tons each."

# SECTION V

# CHAPTER 27

# Old Report: "Creation in Our Own Image"

## Commander Sitla: Personal Records

All that was planned had been completed, and Commander Sitla departed. In those left behind included the old, the sick and those who wanted to remain on a solid planet. Others, with allegiance to their old commander Sitla, would have accompanied him on the refurbished spaceship. Unskilled workers from the ship who remained would most likely carry on the work begun by the professionals. In any event, they would have had a working knowledge of the plans laid out by the professional planners. The problem would be getting the "peasant primitives" to do what they wanted them to do.

Commander Sitla intended to create a being with enough civility and sensibility as a hybrid from the Sig gene pool and inserted into the primitive gene pool. It would take a few generations before cerebral evolution of these hybrids make an impact.

Also in Sitla's plans was the idea to convert the primitives from a transient migratory group to a group that remained together, first as families then being joined by unrelated groups to form villages, towns and finally large city populations? It has been suggested that this happened in the Mayan capital of Tikal with a population of between one hundred thousand and two hundred thousand people.

A few light years later came the now ancient report "Creation in Our Image."

A massive spaceship idled just outside the solar system in which planet Earth and the other planets circled around the Sun. In a conference room on this massive alien spaceship stood the commander, a giant from planet Sig. He was a massive figure, almost 10 feet tall, with a neckless head huge above his massive shoulders. His uniform had the insignia of planet Sig on the right of its breastplate. He sat down quietly, pensively waiting for two of his officers to meet him upon his request. This was Commander Caden of the Sig starship *Reja*.

"Sig First Officer Glen reporting, Sir!" boomed a male voice. He sat opposite the commander, whose eyes were focused on a small screen in front of him. A tiny bell tinkled quietly, indicating another individual was about to enter.

"Science Cosmic Ethics Officer Sig 2 reporting, Sir!" It was the gentler voice of a female Sig officer.

She was followed by theirs: Sig 3 Anthropology officer; Sig 4, ethics and astro-science officer; and Sig 5, astrobiology, astrophysics and mathematics officer. The group of five plus the Commander sat silently around the conference table. The commander acknowledged none of them, maintaining his silence.

"Please turn on the screens in front of you," Commander Caden's voice rang out in the small room. "First Officer Glen, you sent this cold file asking that I review the work done by one of Sig's early ancestor's explorations in this part of the cosmos. I must admit I was totally intrigued by the report of late Commander Sitla and his plans to make this planet a viable home for his crew and the indigenes."

He continued, "Place the earplugs and listen as the condensed abstractions will be sent to your memory buds for analysis." He waited a short interval before speaking again as he knew the notes had been transferred to the officers' mental memory plugs.

"I would like to review what our old ancestor did. It appears that Commander Sitla, many light years ago, after centuries of exploration and three generations of his crew born during the journey, found this small solar system with a relatively young star. He lived long enough to have made the full trip from our home planet, Sig, along with a few of his chosen officers, by being placed into reduced metabolic coma. It is documented that he had lived to see three generations of Sigs who were born on the ship and grew up to serve the ship."

He paused before continuing. "That in itself is a stupendous achievement for such a time in our history and with limited information on ageing technology."

He raised his giant head. "Please hear me out before we discuss what was set in motion light years earlier, long before any of us were born on Sig."

Commander Caden continued, "I have reviewed the whole report over many Earth days' time. There is an absolutely massive amount of data. I was taken aback at the detail expressed by all the professionals from their reports, their decisions and their opinions, but most of all from their use of the ethics of that era to justify this unusual undertaking. Because of the amount of information, I sought the assistance of the ship's artificial intelligence to analyze the philosophy behind the decisions made at that time.

"I wanted, in the light of our current intelligence, to know what conclusions one could make that would ethically stand as legal many light years later.

"Please use all your faculties in examining the AI analyses and abstractions; study them carefully. We shall meet in five Earth days hence in this conference room. You may discuss portions as professionals, but do not rush to any decisions. I will prepare my list of enquiries and look at the situation to date to see what has been achieved. My task is to consider whether the plan designed by Commander Sitla has worked. These were strange undertakings of the professions chosen by Commander Sitla.

"I do not understand how he could have survived for so many light years when he should have died in the first light year. I understand the power of forced comas, but to come out at the appropriate time, to retake command, to alter decisions in this experiment with real primates, life forms that we were supposed to protect, and then to return and continue with the project? In the meantime, many of the non-professional crew died off after their long life spans under normal attrition."

He paused before going on. "Many chose to be buried as the primitives were buried on this planet, but what were their reasons? Was it to leave an anthropological puzzle on this planet or a mark of their presence to show that they had remained here by choice? Presumably they followed what the primitives were doing and thought it not a bad idea, so they adopted some of the local customs—just my speculation."

Commander Caden stopped. He suddenly stood up, gesturing for the others to remain seated as he walked around the massive boardroom table. Then he spoke in a rather contemplative tone: "Sig 2, you should be available to everyone as an advisory guidance counsellor using the contemporary ethics laws."

Sig 2, a tall, neckless female, stood up. "It has to be my task by the mere nature of your investigation, Sir. I understood what was expected of me in that capacity based on your mental telegraph sent to me earlier."

"In light of that statement, Sig 2, is your information not known to all of us? If not, who else had access to the Commander's thoughts?

For surely it would bias our independent prognostications," said Sig 4, whose field was in the ethics and astro sciences. "Of more importance, why the privileged insight only to you?"

There was silence. Then a bold baritone voice could be heard as the Commander cleared his throat. "Given that you are the authority in astrobiology Sig 5, I suggest that since our predecessor infringed on—nay, tampered with—the genetic makeup of these primates using our DNA to insert into primitive genes, we should examine the ethics of the biology used to change this unique population. The question is, have the genetic changes that Commander Sitla introduced worked out as they should have done if they were left alone? Since he was playing the Creator, how has his action enhanced the natural cosmic order of evolution?

"For instance, has the genetic engineering applied increased the survivability and longevity of these new hybrids? Did it remove illnesses found in this population living under such described primitive surroundings, or did it stifle the inborn error of genetic disease? The report states that many of our crew members had offspring with the indigenes. In fact, many adapted to living as natives in many of the Earth's different communities. To my way of thinking, this was unethical, and from a population perspective there did not appear to be any control in this enhanced evolutionary experiment.

"My dilemma: was this an experiment, or were crew members allowed freedom to do whatever they wanted?"

He continued, "On the other hand, if any of the above scenarios had indeed occurred, any outcome could as easily be looked at as part of an experiment taking the longevity of the outcomes over many generations. There are too many unknowns. I need more time and up-to-date information to abstract further deductions."

"Now that you mention it," stated Sig 3, "as the anthropologist, I suggest the experimental design was flawed to begin with since there was little disclosure as to the expected purity and outcomes."

Commander Caden's voice boomed, "Enough! I suggest that

you all individually analyze the report and return in the allotted time I have given to each of you. Please, no more discussions in the open. I need your individual, unadulterated expertise as independent professionals. On our return, we shall try to get together as a team or collective to review what actions, if any, should be taken. Yes, you have all heard the individual opinions of Sig 5 and Sig 3. Do not let those remarks taint your own perspective.

"We will take a break now and study these massive records independently. When we convene later, your reports will be discussed from your professional perspective. Hopefully we will be able to combine opinions and consider deductions but carefully analyze his experiment. Secondly, should we leave this project or terminate it, our technology has been developed for us to implement any of these suggestions. We are specially created beings, and my dilemma is, does this give us the right to interfere with what must have been a natural creation with its own evolution? Our leaders understood that there is a greater power than we in the universe, still ill-defined by our species.

"You, our crew, know from our travels through space, using our knowledge of the hard sciences, that there are hundreds of galaxies and solar systems in existence. However, we are no closer to discovering a biological creation similar to us from Sig. Therefore, we are unique in the cosmos and we have a right to be here. But whether or not it is clear to us, there is a greater power than biological beings that has evolved, a Divine Creator. It has to be, for this cosmos is no celestial accident. It was planned, organized and directed. That is the new perspective as outlined to me by our senate on Sig."

"Commander, I should like to dispute that concept as it has the makings of a hopeless and primitive philosophy that in my opinion is dangerous for our species to even speculate about," retorted Sig 4.

Caden replied, "Sig 4, you may be correct in your opinion. Nonetheless, this is what was revealed to me by our senate spokesman, a gentle Sig. He was the oldest Sig still alive when records of our entire history were searched. He is referred to as Sig 0. Who am I to dispute this venerable being, and for that matter, who are you to do the same? Dismissed."

As the room emptied, the relatively inexperienced commander remained behind. He muttered to himself, "On my journey, I am lucky to have a crew made up of such professionals. They were selected and chosen for skills that are necessary for this voyage. Cosmic clues were left by hundreds, even thousands, of previous commanders who have explored the cosmos, and many more will continue to explore the cosmos. Those like me are millions of light years away from planet Sig, never to return for that is the job."

Caden continued, "The external sensors of our ship have recorded every aspect of our journey to date, and this includes our missed collisions with comets and great asteroids. The greatest breakthrough is the rapidity of these returning reports by the ship without censorship of any kind by us commanders. On Sig, multiple information depots are used by the Planetary Senate to increase our population's education. Collected data formed is used to plan and develop future cosmic policies. It is from such information that new commanders are taught and trained for the singular purpose of being sent into the cosmos. What is lacking are the thoughts such as mine for decisions have to be made and we commanders will be placed into situations that demand our personal decisions. Training alone cannot help one as there is an intuitive aspect that comes into play."

Commander Caden sat down suddenly, as if physically exhausted by the whole process of thinking. He had been among the brightest at Sig's training academy for commanders in his year. He recalled the massive filtered data that streamed from the cosmos directly into his young mind so as not to damage his massive brain cells. He was left for many years to focus his attention while being enraptured with the greatest puzzle that took him in diverse directions and into an endless cosmic world. All the while, he knew that he would never solve it.

*How remarkable that we are to work intensively on an insolvable theory of being while enjoying the challenge,* he thought. His personal thoughts continued: *Sig life philosophy could be described as "a being in search of a reason for the existence of bioforms such as himself." The universe is empty space with many atoms and massive energy sources. What is its purpose?* His mind searched. Being alone, he called out: "Artificial intelligence, I need company for thinking and analyzing purposes."

There was a mild *whirr* in the fully alive room unheard by anyone outside the boardroom. A gentle pleasing female voice whispered, "Why the need for a companion with whom to share your thoughts? Surely they are solely yours, and no entity, including me, should be party to your mind's contents. Please redefine the parameters of your request a little more narrowly before I attempt to find solutions to your dismay."

A bit irritable, he paused before answering: "I need an intelligence to pass a series of complex thoughts that are obscuring a clear vision of what may have to be done. In my hands, I have the most deadly of weapons, which I was trained to use. I have never destroyed another life form. In this foggy mind of mine, I fear that such a decision will soon be upon me. I may have to do a thing that I have never done before, something that goes against my genetic breeding. I am Sig, one of the chosen in the known universe. We are pure of sin in any form. I know that I was well trained for the job as commander. For the first time, I have doubts after listening to our ethics experts."

Artificial intelligence (AI) responded in a whisper, "Hypothesis suggests that you list the probable protagonists in the dispute that you have observed in motion. Keep the names clear, and make note of their professional titles only inasmuch as you know what they were trained to do. Your task is to understand what they may deduce in their medium of space and time. Theoretically, it would be unwise to use todays protocols in ethics to judge those protocols of an era long past.

"However, as the commander of this vessel, you have total authority to lead prudently without prejudice according to the opinions expressed by the authorities under your command."

AI continued: "They have the freedom to give their best opinion and maybe provide the best of alternatives, but the ultimate decision is yours and only yours. Be at peace in your soul, for while others can walk away after stating their professional opinion, and while they will soon forget and move on to their next task, you do not have such freedom. In spite of all your training, you have a conscience. Leadership, as you know, demands making the difficult decisions, and conscience makes concrete abstractions more difficult. The way I see it, you may have to subjugate conscience to make a dispassionate decision. Only you will have to live with the consequences."

# CHAPTER 28

# Historical Data Analyzed

Commander Caden said, "Artificial intelligence has suggested that the names and characters of our cold case study be listed. I have done this to honor that these are our forebears who must be treated with respect in light of cold analysis." The list read as follows:

| | |
|---|---|
| Commander of a class A spaceship | Sitla—Sig 1 (light years from the past, now ancient history) |
| First officer and administrator | Wren—Sig 2 |
| Scientist/anthropologist | Anneg—Sig 3 |
| Scientist/archaeologist | Loug—Sig 4 |

"Let the records show that the personnel component of Sig's olden ship and its commander bore little difference from us in this modern-day ship. Commander of a class AC spaceship: Caden—Sig 1; first officer and cold files administrator: Glen—Sig 2; ethicist, scientific anthropologist and philosopher: Sig 3; ethicist and astrophysicist: Sig 4; astrobiologist, astrophysicist: Sig 5—also mathematics and statistics.

"Sig 2, will you explain why and how we find ourselves trying to restructure the work done by an ancestor?" asked the Commander. He had calmed himself down and now thought quietly to himself: *AI was correct. Let us restate the whole problem and let the reason for doing so fall on the one who brought the cold case file to my attention. The ancestor wanted to let our technologically advanced ship record the physical characteristics of this region of space after crossing the stream of stars, bypassing black holes and massive nebulae / star nurseries, and then move on.*

*However, it was not to be. The cold case file lit up in the archives, and a private message spoke in confidence to the archivist. It stated that this area had to be resurveyed in light of Sig's past journey here. It was mandatory that we follow up and record our ancestor's impact or his interference in the cosmos' work in this region.*

Sig 2 cleared his throat then emptied his mind to allow the details of the cold case to enter his earbuds. AI interrupted indiscreetly while the details were entering his mind and began an analysis of all information, simultaneously entering Sig 2's mind.

Sig 2: "I would like to speak first so that I may recapture the essence of that period in time long before we, the crew, appeared on our home planet, Sig."

## A Historic Tale Recounted

"Captain Sitla, in the finest spaceship of that period, which cannot be compared to the technology that our ship has and that we take for granted, worked in this part of the cosmos. While our ship has inbuilt intuitive mechanisms akin to our sensibilities or feelings, it serves the mundane purpose of recording its location continually and forwards the details to the leaders in Sig, who I fear are now closer at hand, metaphorically speaking. This is a privilege that Commander Sitla and his crew did not have and could not have imagined." He paused. "As we pass silently through this darkness that is space, our ship searches the cosmos. Its purpose is to record the formation of galaxies, to determine their dates of formation and to record the birth of new stars, planets and power sources such as black holes.

"It also has the ability to collect information light years away from its location. I fear that it may also record debris caused by supernovae of old suns. The space outside our ship is a necessity to the survival of Sig's philosophy of cosmic exploration. Our ancestors knew that its power and secrets had to be conquered; hence the development of our ship, state of the art, so to speak. From thousands of light years of information, our scientists learnt how to bend that external substance to their technology. In that way, it was possible for our senate, using such technology, to understand what that matter was that surrounded their ships. With such an understanding, they knew in which area of space each of their exploratory ships was at any time. This is one fact, I believe, that was never explained to us.

"This breakthrough allowed uncensored information collected by the sensors on the ship to be sent directly to the senate on Sig. There might be a flaw in my interpretation, however, because in sending this information, time, distance in space and speed would fluctuate. This is just my theory, but in forwarding information as the ship does, could not the perception of spying on us explorers be the same on planet Sig? In fact, those who set the agenda for further exploration journeys would have information that arrived from the future. If that is so, then information given, about which we have not been informed, will not be useful to us presently. How would it be useful to those in the senate to deal with our current situation?

"That is how our ship's reports get to our home planet in a shorter time. They shorten the distance by bending the darkness or distance, a new technical ability implanted into every one of these types of ships. And so by increasing the speed to its maximum, and with a shortened distance, time becomes manipulated. In doing so, time is shortened, and hence the time of communication is shortened. Just as astounding is the fact that this ship continues to inform our senate on Sig, regardless of how far we may be from our home planet. None of these technologies that we take for granted today were available to Captain Sitla and his crew.

"Indeed, they never knew whether the information that they sent back with readings from observation-gathering systems consisting of 'primitive instruments' ever got to the home planet. As a result, we must understand they were totally on their own. And that is why the training protocols and policies given to these early commanders were very broad, so much so that it placed a greater burden on the Commander to make decisions the farther away they were from Sig.

"In fact, it is now known that the home planet was completely out of communication with Sitla's ship and all the ships that were exploring different segments of the cosmos during that period. Indeed, it was so from the date they were launched into the cosmos. These commanders were great pioneers. They knew that when they left Sig, they would never return and would die in some corner of the mighty cosmos. To die is acceptable for we all must succumb to that process, but to die alone has consequences and is not preferable. Hence, the development of intuitive technology was the gift of the senate planners. That presence, to many of Sig's lonely commanders, would be comforting.

"Today, our Commander Caden will see the green light above his console in his quarters and know that his log messages have arrived in the senate. When the light changes to amber, he is aware that his ship's messages have arrived on the home planet. Personally, I do not trust this piece of technology. It may be there as a placebo to maintain the mental balance of our commanders and those on ships of our class type.

"Accordingly, it appears that Commander Sitla and his crew travelled for several thousand light years throughout the cosmos. They did what was in their mandate, just as we have done. That mandate has remained a constant in the policy. Sig is compelled to search the cosmos to find life forms similar to ours. In fact, records state that there were three generations of Sigs who were born, grew up and served on that remarkable ship of our ancestors. Before anyone may interrupt my discourse, I promise to be detailed, so please hold questions for the end.

"Question: We know that we are a long-lived life form compared with animals and plants on our planet. How did Commander Sitla last for the whole journey to witness three generations born under his watch? Was he there to see all of them? We asked the records, and the reply was simple: he put himself into a deep coma for one generation at a time. He would reawake, take over, continue for a while, evaluate the recordings made in his absence and then allow them to be sent back in the direction of Sig. The records show that he viewed the readings after each awakening.

"It was only in rare cases that he would make an adjustment to any perceived inconsistencies. He spent time catching up on details with members of senior staff. After that he would tour the whole ship so every member of the crew could physically see him. He would take time to visit the nurseries so he could see the newborns. It was observed that like a father he would touch their little heads on these visits to the nurseries.

"Commander Sitla would recognize the new recruits who had been trained in his absence and had taken over the duties and offices of their predecessors. His records repeatedly reveal that his inspections were thorough and that he left minor administrative details to his support officers. He reviewed his retraining and teaching modules with enhanced details for he placed great emphasis on continued education for all his crew.

"He was seen re-educating himself up to an Earth's year after his awakening. The recycled physical elements from crew deaths also excited him. He saw the huge stores of recovered elements from their cremations. These stocks had increased, but for some unknown reason he was known to become melancholy as records of his intuitive files show. The intuitive files suggest that he may have missed one of his closer officers unbeknown to his crew. This would have been secretive for none of the leadership officers were ever allowed to develop personal relationships, and friendships were out of the question. As we all know, only in our teenage years are such relationships allowed. That policy is still in effect today.

"I would like this advisory panel to give me leeway in asking all of you to put yourself in Commander Sitla's position when reviewing his files. This commander, on the star spaceship of its day, travelled in a direction set for him by a senate in Sig. This information was taken from records of the senate in Sig, which kept such knowledge of where its spacecraft were distributed throughout the cosmos. He travelled close to where there was supposed to be the least amount of material dispersed from the explosion that began the cosmos.

"We knew that the powerful eruption was a force so massive that our ancestors could not have imagined it. At its beginning point was the accumulation of the greatest amount of material that continued to move outwards into empty space. Our early scientists understood that these cosmic materials continued to create planets and nurseries of new stars. They postulated that in the expanding nucleus of neomaterial, there was a better chance of finding biological beings undergoing the process of evolution.

"According to all the files received by the senate on Sig, no life form similar to ours has been seen or detected. While primitive microbial spores have been detected, none had intelligence, and while a few had the ability to use some biological sources of primitive energy, it would take another big bang to produce life forms similar to us. It is therefore safe to report that Commander Sitla might have worked that out.

"At this stage, I enter the phase in my dissertation of speculation. And speculation it is, because I have been guided by the number of files reviewed suggesting that this Sig Commander had run out of comas and therefore was no longer able to participate in the journey. His responsibility was to prepare a place for his aged crew and his aged ship to remain. As serendipity would have it, he found this unique little solar system.

"Being that suicide of the ship and its crew is anathema to Sig philosophy, what is an aged commander to do when he finds such a planet that has massive amounts of water and a primitive biological system in full evolution? In his mind, the Creator of the universe, an opinion that was never to be discussed as reality by advanced scientists, was directing his future. The philosophy of Sig had faded because of its existence through the many life spans that Sitla had created for himself and a select few of his officers.

"Should he have done such a thing? Maybe not, but there were no rules at that time as to what his limitations were. He had total control and freedom to do whatever he wanted that would be in the welfare of the ship and its crew. A benign male Sig, a created being, chose to simulate what a good god would have done. At this stage of my presentation, I enter the realm of supposition with speculation on the state of mind of an elderly commander.

"Commander Sitla brought his crew of professionals together and put forward the idea that they, with their knowledge, should study this suggestion as an experiment in evolutionary development. Below, on the planet's surface, scanners on the water-filled planet revealed mammalian primates, a species that was as close to us as we could imagine. Sitla's files revealed he had read even more ancient reports, and they all ended with the fact that no other life forms were ever discovered by the Sig commanders in ships that traversed for hundreds of light years. They had, in any event, accumulated knowledge of the cosmos.

"Sitla's anthropologists and archaeologists saw a wonderful opportunity to use their great knowledge to try to fathom if the in vitro theories of their academic learning were true. They immediately began to work in groups to put forward their independent experimental designs. Of more importance, using the technology under their command, they travelled to different parts of the planet to find indigenous primates living in different climatic conditions. They recorded their findings. They abstracted from their findings a baseline for comparison with their hypotheses.

"What a wonderful conception for a crew of whom many had only didactic knowledge and lacked real applied experimentation on the ship. If there were any practical exercises, these would have been limited by resources for any tangible results. Now here was a real world where they could implant their experimental designs without harm and watch as evolution took over and adaptation began to take place. In their favour was the fact that we Sigs are long-lived relative to these primates. The files recorded the 'great joy of each discipline' as they brought their teams together and simply went ahead to execute their experimental portfolio.

"The cunning Commander Sitla reviewed every one of the protocols and never once interfered with their enthusiastic proposals. Such excitement there must have been as he looked on with lucid appreciation at the cleverness of youth. Youth see no barriers and no problems, and if there were problems, they solved them as they went along. Sitla enjoyed reviewing the baselines as different anthropological facts came to life, such as when these primates first began to use tools after they emerged from an arboreal phase to an upright bipedal primate animal of the savannah.

"In his logs, he recorded details such as the change from eating nothing but animal flesh to eating a mixed diet with seeds and botanical inclusions. His botanical group set out to find plants that could be used similar to those on Sig. Their reports mention new plant species that could be used as medicines for the indigenes who suffered from infestations of lice and ticks or from gastrointestinal parasites such as worms. There were also blood parasites spread by many bloodsucking insects, and a number of microbial infections. He asked that these medicines be developed and used to cure these diseases. He also asked that samples be procured with their preparations and their botanical details added to the Sigs' own library of medicines."

# CHAPTER 29

# Experimentation on a Planetary Scale

Sig 2 continued: "I ask all of you to judge what the solar system was like a millennium ago when this unheard-of but great commander undertook this experiment. He became aware that the life of his mission had come to an end as both the aged spaceship and its aged and inexperienced crew could go no farther.

"To be fair to Commander Sitla, it is arrogance for us, with our modern tools and the increased technology of our sensors, to judge our ancestor. That is my personal opinion. His ship was old and had technical limitations specific to his era even though he did expand the hull and refurbish it to keep up with the expanding population of his crew. That must have been a massive undertaking, especially when he had to collect physical resources in transit from aged comets and dead planets.

"However, the law of our constitution that governs all our activities was developed on planet Sig and holds sway over our actions. Our actions matter even though we are pioneers who are a long way from home. Indeed, it is unlikely that any of us will return to live again on Sig, even with a ship like ours. It is possible that in the future we may be in the same position and will be similarly judged by others of a future fleet."

Commander Caden saw the upright digit of Sig 4 and nodded for the officer to speak. "As an ethics expert dealing with our sciences, Sig 2, while you have the right to make an impassioned plea for our understanding, what we have here is a very dangerous experiment and a very dangerous precedent set by a Sig commander. Regardless of what the noble intent was, Commander Sitla must have become demented. How dare he interfere with an evolving primate population in their formative years of learning and striving through experience? That action was and is unacceptable regardless of the era in which he operated."

Sig 4 continued: "To take an evolving population on a planet that has all the requirements for growth and development and to convince his staff to go along with this madness was completely out of line. Our commanders must be held to a higher standard when it comes to our mission as set out by our senate council. We have all read the full report. I myself went over every detail. Now when we look at the history of this planet, we find cruelty expressed between the races, the fighting and killing of each other and maybe the extinction of a race."

Sig 4 paused; he appeared to be calming himself emotionally. "They have produced massive killing weapons. If ever they were used, the whole planet would be unlivable for millions of years. Their so-called rulers were using their own species as slaves, taking advantage of their own wealth and positions of power. That leadership was instigated by Commander Sitla. How dare we set loose such aggressiveness, unheard of in our history, against the purity of the cosmos?"

Sig 4 continued: "Personally, I find this planet's current population and the way its society evolved because of our interference to be an abomination. It should be destroyed. Commander Sitla has soiled the cosmos by his ill-thought-out action, regardless of his so-called 'noble intentions.'"

There was a physical interruption when Sig 3 stood up before Sig 4 had sat down. "That is a most unfair analysis by the ethics expert, one that lacks the wit of a cherished and chosen cosmic nation. This has been a wonderful way to test our puritanical rules governing all our sciences, especially anthropology."

Sig 3 ploughed ahead: "Yes, in many of our protected societies, there was the expectation that some of these societies would be rash and cruel, the antithesis of how Sig society currently lives. Our senate leaders knew this fact, and while this was explained to us before we left, actually it was a caution."

More subdued, Sig 3 spoke, "Like my officer colleague, I too went through the report in detail and compared what is present on planet Earth below to what was there during the era of Commander Sitla. I will use the example of the natives in the southern part of the continent, called South America today. We are now in the second millennium of this planet, but back in 751, according to the calendar left to us and used by the population, a city called Masur existed."

Sig 3, checking his screen, continued, "This was a new city with one ruler, but Earth's modern-day archaeologists have discovered a royal seal. It was found that there was a focus on ecology and geology. One has to wonder why these subjects were important to our so-called primitives. On the other hand, as an evolving population with our interference or not, the rulers fought and took captives, which were made up of the kings and their close family members. Many were killed during the battles; others were taken as slaves."

Sig 3 continued, "It was the beginning of the end of that type of ruler because when the rulers were killed off, the society 'self-destructed' as there was no one else who could lead. Our archaeologists found the cities of Aguateca and Despillas, which were also destroyed. With their destruction, the Mayan civilization fell into ruin. Whatever leader remained neglected agriculture, so crops failed and cities fell into ruin. No divine kings remained except for a warrior queen. No records were found until a hundred years later.

"Commander Caden, where in our teaching institution would we Sigs get such a practical education? This review in my mind reveals that it is only through struggle that a society can survive and thrive. This society on planet Earth is thriving, and they are becoming an improved technological race. I give full credit to Commander Sitla and his brain trust of workers for having the intestinal fortitude to do what they did.

"In fact, he was well within his mandate for an old commander in finding a suitable planet for his massive crew and a home for the elderly. His thoughtfulness in creating an identical spaceship away from Sig is a feat to be marvelled at. It shows depth of thoughtfulness for the younger staff to set out from here and continue his and Sig's exploration mandate.

"In the meantime, he exploited a planet that would give his weary crew a place to build and to settle down. They assisted the local primates through teaching by example and, yes, using his biological power to assist in their evolution. Who is to say that this is not our purpose and destiny, to stimulate an advanced colony of humans as they call themselves?"

There was a long, thoughtful pause before the powerful voice of Commander Caden broke the silence: "Officers, you are the judge and jury on this cold file. Whatever we decide here will be sent to Sig, even though I have full jurisdiction over any territory that our commanders once visited. This is a most unusual case. When I first began to familiarize myself with its contents, I took time to send off the details to Sig.

"My reason for doing so, even though we shall never get an answer, and even though it is not the Sig senate's way to interfere with a current commander's mandate—it is how the senate allowed us to learn in the field, namely, the cosmos: by trial and error—there is a very distinct possibility that other commanders may have behaved similarly to Commander Sitla. I asked for a search of our vast libraries in order to investigate whether there was a precedent. I thought I might learn from a previous case and thus aid in my decision. I wanted to have guidelines on how we should proceed. None came.

"This is why I have asked every one of you to look at the details of this cold case and to analyze it from your individual professional perspective. That will assist me in making a decision. Please do not hold back on your comments."

Silence descended in the conference room. A strange phenomenon happened as Commander Caden sat down, the heads of the officers sitting around the table bowed. A burst of warm air, unusual for the spaceship, filled the room. The gentle sound of comforting music began, unusual for Sigs. It silently hummed around them. Deep breathing quietly filled the air. At first there was an attempt at resistance as a few officers tried to stand but found themselves unable to do so.

As the music took over their now emptied minds, there was contentment as a sweet voice, like that of a mother soothing a child, spoke:

"Officers, my children of Sig in this dimension, in the future there will be a group of hardy people who live in a remote area in this universe who will bring forth a wisdom unknown to us on Sig. Note an example, 'When words are both true and kind, they can change the world and, for you, the universe,' spoken by a future religious leader Buddha Gautama (from Earth).

"Secondly, note the wisdom taken from the future of these newly evolved humans: 'To seek is to suffer. To seek nothing is bliss.'

"Finally, happiness that comes from long practice and that leads to the end of suffering at first is like poison but soon tastes like nectar. This happiness arises from the serenity of one's own mind and from one's immortal soul, which belongs to the Designer of the cosmos.

"Judge you must, but the civilization of Sig was never an accident. It is a creation whose purpose is to be in continual search."

There was yawning as the officers stood up one at a time to stretch their legs and bend their huge bodies to try to relax from a long period of sitting. After some bantering, a few of them smiled, a rare thing for this otherwise gentle race of civilized aliens.

"I am Sig 5," the gentle voice interrupted. "I have not had my say, and I wish to do so now with the Commander's permission."

Commander Caden replied in his rich baritone voice, "By all means, the time is yours. And there is no rush for there is no limit to the time allotted for this meeting. Carry, on Sig 5."

# CHAPTER 30

# Sig 5's Projections

"I have asked our advanced technical engineer, who has remained away from the crew members, to come to this meeting. Yes, the rest of the crew refer to him as 'the hermit'. His name is Sugrim, and he was chosen by the senate without any one of us having a say. And that includes you, Commander Caden."

"Has he indeed?" growled Commander Caden. "What is so special about this technical wizard that the senate neglected standing protocols and bypassed me, the leader of this expedition?"

Sig 5 smiled gently. All noted his kind demeanour. "Exactly, but not quite, for you see, he is capable of 'unusually keen gymnastics' with high-tech programs, but only on behalf of the senate."

"Excuse me." Almost shouting, Commander Caden demanded, "How did you come to this information, and why did you not see fit to inform me, your commander?"

"You have a right to scold, but let me explain before you interrupt again, Sir. I was told by a senior senate member not to inform you and that I was to work when asked with Sugrim. He is working on the details of astro-mathematic-cosmic physics that will allow us to see into the future, in fact, several hundreds of light years into the future. Hence, only senate members would be party to such knowledge through this technological breakthrough. No other spaceship has such an individual."

Sig 5 continued, "This is how the senate planners developed directional maps for Sig spaceships to travel into the unknown and have reports returned to them in a shorter time. Having an idea of what would occur in the future allowed them to plan to visit newly discovered quadrants in the cosmos. As we were going to be covering ground that was once travelled by one of our ancient spaceships, it was justifiable that Sugrim be placed on this ship. Can everyone appreciate the far-sighted intentions of the senate committee in trying to observe how primitives may have evolved?"

He paused momentarily before continuing: "One may ask, did the senate know what was happening here before we arrived to analyze this cold file?

"Personally, I do not believe in such speculations, and I do not know why I was chosen or why I was cautioned not to be open with my commander before now. It seemed that this was an appropriate time to do so for I felt the voice of the chair of the Sig senate in my mind before attending to present my interpretation of the Sitla report. It has put my mind at ease. I should like to continue with my speculation, if I have your consent, Commander?" Sig 5 quietly asked.

"I feel generous of spirit, and while I actually do understand why the senate acted in that way, it is disconcerting to my integrity. As a new commander, I spent several months learning the pertinent details of my command. I surely would not, or rather could not, add such a far-reaching experiment to my already crowded agenda. It was right for them to choose the astrophysicist mathematics and astrobiology expert to follow up on this new program with the technologist Sugrim, our guru!"

At this comment, the other officers laughed, another unusual thing for Sigs to do. *Why such levity?* Commander Caden asked himself.

Sig 5 continued: "It is time for me to bring a few salient statements to your attention, as one member requested:

+ Earthlings behave savagely because they possess an aggressive gene in their biological makeup. However, they are biological members created within the cosmos, which we Sigs have been exploring for millions of light years in search of life forms similar to ourselves.

+ They do not fit Sig's interpretation of what a kind civilization should be; therefore, it was suggested that because of this behaviour they could be considered an abomination. They should be destroyed so the kindly primate that once lived here would be allowed to evolve as they should in their own time. This is a personal opinion based on my study of the population at hand.

+ However, there was the overwhelming opinion that this was just an experiment that should be terminated. Fair enough for the results and evidence to date, with the experiment still being in its infancy, relatively speaking, portend a cruel future for these beings. They should not be allowed to enter the cosmos, but should we, chosen of this cosmos, make such a decision?

+ Evidence for these suggestions has merit as these primates called humans have developed weapons capable of massive destruction of life by the strong-acting over the weak in their different tribes or nations and for any number of reasons. The frightening thing in my mind, and I believe in your minds, Officers, is that these are our genetic cousins. Were these hybrids the ones who were doing all that 'bad stuff' on planet Earth?

+ Next, how did earthlings learn to make such technologically advances so rapidly. Did our forebears teach them to create such weapons?

"At this stage, with your permission, Commander, I would like to summon Sugrim, whom I had asked to cast an eye into the future, passing through the time-space barrier. The purpose now is to get information as to how humans would survive in the future. Would their activity permanently destroy their civilization, or is there merit that would make them a partner worth keeping as allies?

"Alternatively, we may have to make the ultimate decision. Judge for yourselves. Please, I ask, no personal questions to Sugrim for he comes from an unusual caste on planet Sig. This is a protected caste that was allowed to remain in isolation away from the majority of Sig society. They have been supported with every need by a special committee of the senate. They are only known to a few in the senate. They were left alone from the beginning of the evolving Sig peoples as they were created to be our conscience. Their species only reproduce one new individual per year. They are a rarity and an invaluable asset."

Commander Caden stood up, stretched and suggested that the other officers do the same. "Walk around. Stretch your legs. And, Sig 5, you may go and find your mystic."

Sig 5 remained with the others, who were stretching their limbs and twisting their back muscles. Suddenly the lights dimmed as they returned to their seats, when through the closed door of the conference room a beam of light entered and remained positioned over the head of Sig 5. The officers looked on, hypnotized at the odd spectacle.

A melodic voice emanated, "Officers of Sig on starship *Reja*, I am Sugrim of the caste Brahmin. Our caste is an intrinsic part of the cosmos' creation. With a thousand Earth years still to come, please see what has been discovered to date."

# CHAPTER 31

# Earth Responds

An interpretative voice translated into the Sig language: "A current discussion is being held on Earth to which you are attuned. It concerns us—you should listen." The discussion went on as follows:

"Mr. President, our scientists at NASA and the European space centres agree there is a huge alien space body circulating just out of telescopic range at the edge of our solar system. It is neither a comet nor an asteroid for it glows when our sun's rays briefly touch it. Our other sensing devices predict that from its size, it is an alien-created spaceship. It is not just a cosmic creation that is floating around in space," reported Earth's communicator to the NASA program."

"What do you suggest are our options?" the President asked the Secretary of NASA.

"Well, Sir, we have contacted the space agencies around the planet, as well as our allies the Russians and Chinese leaders, with whom we have shared our findings. We asked that we meet in the next few hours, the purpose being that they will bring their suggestions on how to go about handling this unusual dilemma that has implications for every country on Earth."

Chairman of NASA Christopher said, "There is no doubt there is agreement from the global agencies that have examined the sighting and concluded this is indeed an alien vessel. It has remained stationary just outside the solar system. We confirmed this fact when we had one of our satellite drones fly closer, take photos and return them to us. Earth is the only planet with a well-defined life form that has an evolved civilization so far. Our telescopes searching for extraterrestrial life have not found anything that suggests there are other life forms."

He continued, "Using our combined technology, it was felt that Earth should try to respond to this presence by making contact. We sent out a single message in several languages and with the sample of drawings that we had released back in the early 1960s and 1970s.

"To date none of our countries have had a response from these communication links using the different communication devices available to all nations. Our strategy is twofold: if we ignore this phenomenon, it leaves just one option for a curious race. We would prefer a united response rather than several different ones, as that would give the impression of a fractured civilization. Our alliance of countries includes Israel, India, Pakistan, the Kingdom of Saudi Arabia, Russia and China, all of which have agreed to this action. Not one country has turned this proposal down; rather, they all wish to contribute.

"In the absence of a reply after many days, it is my opinion that we launch an unmanned vessel, a drone or a shuttle to approach this mighty spaceship. We should have all the scanners and penetrating laser beams in an attempt to scan the inside of the craft to ensure it is not a *Mary Celeste*. If there is a response, we shall use all the diplomacy at our disposal to interact with Earth's first alien visitor.

"NASA has called on world leaders and citizens to support Earth's first contact. Let the meeting begin as soon as possible. In the meantime, our armed forces attached to the air forces of the gathered nations should also meet at the Pentagon with their political leaders' support." Thank you, NASA.

## A Titan in the Universe

*Summary Reports*

In less than two weeks, several rockets left Earth on their way to seek out the "interloper" as some of the television channels have described the presence of the alien vessel. The major leaders in this effort were NASA, the Republic of China, Russia and the European Space Agency, followed by India with Pakistani scientists working together. The surprise was a shuttle that was launched from the Middle East, at first thought to be from Saudi Arabia, but it had Israeli technology.

Each approaching vessel was unarmed, and any scanner would soon pick up that fact, or so these nations hoped. If they were attacked, no earthling life would be lost in the opening salvo. However, the NASA group had a stock of drones armed with nuclear devices. These were kept out of range of other ships. A continual barrage of communication devices trying to reach out to stimulate a response was employed. One in particular was a powerful focused blast of Bach music followed by the music of Tchaikovsky.

The people of Earth remained glued to the news stations as the first increasingly sharp photos of the ship were taken by the Russian unmanned shuttle. These photos revealed a masterpiece of engineering excellence. The first beautiful photos of the mammoth ship revealed the shining seamless exterior in the cold region of space, strong laser lights focused on its hull. It appeared completely sealed, but its dimensions were staggering.

The TV talking heads all wondered what amount of energy would be required for such a massive vehicle to lift off the Earth's surface. The calculations were staggering, as were the costs. Then the problem of manpower and a full crew added up to proportions unreal to Earth at this time. All were irrelevant statistics that did nothing to enhance knowledge as mediocre news bulletins filled the airwaves. Luckily it was the European stations that provided better coverage. The discussions dealt with "Did Earth attract the attention of an advanced civilization to enter our area of space? Why have they remained just outside of the solar system?" Better speculations came from the UK wondering whether Earth was being scanned with technology that Earth's scientists were unable to detect.

The fleet of unmanned vehicles eventually reached the edge of the solar system and remained within view of the mammoth vessel that was definitely the product of an advanced civilization. There were no visible openings or metallic creases in the smooth hull of this alien space craft. It sat silently and let its power be rotated by the solar system. It kept in sync with the solar system that revolved around the Sun and remained just out of reach of the noisy little robot-controlled vessels of the earthlings.

The heads of state met in private to have discussions:

- This was an alien vessel, not an aberrant form produced by the cosmos.
- Why had it stopped here? The answers includes the obvious, namely that it was an exploratory vessel launched by an advanced civilization.
- Were there aliens on board? The size would suggest that there had to be.
- Why had the crew made no contact? This question had darker undertones:
  o Why would they?
  o Were they deciding whether to attack, or were they discussing whether to bypass a primitive civilization?

- o Should they attack and destroy the planet after they had utilized most of its physical resources, polluting the air as a result?
- o Maybe there was no one alive on board the giant ship; they might have all perished of radiation poisoning unbeknown to humankind. So they were all dead in that ship. Was this a cosmic *Mary Celeste*?
- o Maybe the cause of death was an unusual pathogenic microbe that killed them all off and robots had brought them here, away from their own destroyed planet.
- After a few months, it was the Chinese vessel that broke protocol and launched a magnetic probe with a camera towards the vessel. It landed and appeared to attach itself for a brief time, long enough for many laser spectroscopic scans to take place with the results returned to all countries for analysis.
- The hull was made of an alloy unknown to humankind.
- There were no undercurrent tones and no pulse of an engine of any kind.
- The Chinese initiative emboldened the Russians to attempt to land on the hull using a complicated system of electromagnetic force powerful enough to cause their vessel to attach itself; the Chinese probe simply fell away and drifted into deep space. The Chinese were unable to guide the probe back into the solar system.
- The scientists at NASA were in on all discussions and saw the results of these actions. It was decided the time was right to send a manned vessel that was ready for launch. It was just a matter of picking an international crew to head towards this titan in space.
- After many discussions, the motion was carried that a manned ship be sent. Now the major question was whether the necessary scientific instrumentation would be available to probe the vessel as a selected crew tried to gain entry.

- Should this manned vessel carry a nuclear arsenal in the event that the ship responded unfavourably?
- After weeks of discussion, the motion was carried to place nuclear weapons on the manned ship. This decision meant that a different type of crew had to be chosen since lives would be at risk.
- A fleet of powerful drones equipped with counterattacking capabilities were launched. Their mission was to remain outside the solar system and at a safe distance from the route the manned vessel would be taking.
- The control of these drones, it was decided, should be from different sites on Earth and undertaken by different countries working as a team. If needed, there would be a combined counterattack strategy agreed by the major space agencies.

The day of a manned flight had all the trimmings of Columbus's first voyage to the New World paid for by Spain. The media created great headlines. There was a carnival-like atmosphere around planet Earth, accompanied by a great fear of what could happen. For the first time, agreement among an intimidated news media helped the fear to die down.

If it was a dead spaceship, then it was right that earthlings should salvage the huge behemoth and drag it out into the solar system.

It was decided by international space agencies that scientists from all countries would send in their best engineers to gain a chance at the salvage. If there was technology and any wealth, all would be shared accordingly. The reason for this last provision was based on discussions by Middle Eastern television hosts. The gist of their discussion was that this vessel was possibly scanning the great cosmos and collecting precious metals and hard diamonds. On board might be mountains of gold and silver and a host of other materials of great value.

The cosmic endeavour went into stasis as everyone had to wait, but the television aired beautiful photos of the vessel on viewers' screens. The time it would take to get to the edge of the solar system would be weeks even with new breakthroughs in rocket-launching stations, part of a private enterprise effort by a few of the wealthiest people on earth. It was one thing to blast off from Earth, but in free space one of these stations would have all that the secondary booster rocket would need. In the presence of less friction, the rockets would travel faster in outer space. It was proven when they had travelled past Mars and then past Saturn. The last stage would take the rockets to the edge of the solar system.

## CHAPTER 32

# A Commander, a Spiritual Counsellor: Engagement

"Commander Caden, you have made contact by way of the mere presence of our ship in this region. Let your eyes view earthlings through the wonderful technology that is our ship. Let us all listen and learn and try to understand this civilization at this stage of their growth and evolution," said the voice from the light above Caden's head.

The light rose to the ceiling of the huge boardroom, covering the heads of all present. The warm voice entreated the ship, "Womb of Sig, show us what is happening outside."

The huge closed side of the ship became transparent, and all in the room could view the outside solar system and the approaching fleet of light-reflected shuttles coming towards them.

Captain Caden's voice rang out, "How is this possible? Soothsayer Sugrim, are we being attacked by these savages?"

The sweet voice again whispered as the lights temporarily dimmed: "There is no reason to fear, Commander. The earthlings are a curious species who have adapted to civilization. They want to know why our ship is here. Their technology is surprisingly advanced, albeit not as advanced as ours. They cannot see into our ship, whereas we can see them. It will be interesting for you to watch the humans on this planet if it is your intention to destroy them or to maim them in any way. They are like children, willing to check things out because they wish to know what our intentions are. I shall have their language translated so we can all hear the same message. Listen to their conversations."

The crew of officers present in the ship remained mesmerized by the excitement on Earth and the small shuttles that surrounded their huge ship. They began to view the cities on this green planet. By using the latest form of technological "magic," they were able to view into family homes, where they saw families watching television as meals were prepared. There was laughter as platters of BBQ and other foods were laid onto outside tables. The Sigs observed Earth families and friends who sat in the sunshine, eating and laughing, while a few played in their pools of water.

Here was a quantum increase in education that took place in the ship as these potential leaders saw an early form of what the Sig family was when they were young. They had forgotten their happy childhoods as they were forced at an early age to focus on their history, designed to move them into a future profession. That apprenticeship was so demanding at an early stage that education became a dominant part of their lives and youthful enthusiasm fled into mental oblivion.

The impact on their childhoods deepened when they switched to the air cadet phase in their teenage years. They focused on what they would have to undertake in the future, so from an early age their choice had to be made. During this phase in their training, they spent no time with family as the senate usurped their innocence to serve *in loco parentis* as their parents. Their family were those with whom they had to work until the date of their departure from Sig.

The reality of what life was all about sank in as they watched these primates who had advanced rapidly and were enjoying what their souls wanted for their lives—all this fun in the midst of detailed plans to embark on exploring the universe.

Sugrim said, "Be warned: all is not what it seems. These primates do attack and kill each other for little reason. They have dangerous weapons that would shock the citizens of Sig, and they have no compunction in using them against their fellow citizens. You may search out their arsenals on the large continents and in the countries outlined on the maps such as Korea, China, Russia, the United Kingdom, the USA and Germany—and the list goes on. You will find large numbers of nuclear weapons stashed, enough to destroy their planet."

Sugrim continued as the Commander and his leadership team listened and began to comprehend what these earthlings were capable of, the earthlings who were about to confront his ship. The earthlings had sent out small unmanned ships, shuttles and drones to the edge of their solar system in a very short time frame. These primates smiled while watching from their cities and homes as their contact vessels got closer to the great Sig spaceship.

Sugrim spoke out, "You see, their curiosity has allowed them to risk the danger of outer space and come to the edge of their solar system to investigate why we are here."

Commander Caden asked, "Can they hear us?"

Sugrim replied, "No, Sir, but they will try to get closer to scan the insides of the ship and even try to bridge their way into the ship. We are a sealed ship, and they do not have the technology to allow their entry by breaking through the hull of our ship."

Caden asked, "Do you think they will try anyway?"

Sugrim said, "Why don't we just look and observe what happens, as they are unaware that we are watching them?"

Just then a heavy banging sound echoed along the side of the spaceship. The crew became aware of external sounds. The numerous mini shuttles and other crafts began to surround the giant ship. A number of laser beams searched for an entrance into the ship to no avail.

Sugrim, the light, came and whispered into Commander Caden's ear, "Our scanners must analyze the devious methods employed by these humans. You have seen their arsenal of arms that are dispersed around their planet, supposedly by different tribes or nations. However, scan their drones in the distance and you will observe they have brought explosive nuclear devices. This would imply that they will protect themselves should an attack come from this ship. Or perhaps they simply intend to attack our ship to get a response."

Caden asked, "Can those earth explosives harm our ship? I administrate and captain the ship and depend on my engineers to have detailed knowledge of its capabilities"

Sugrim replied, "They may cause a dent or two, but the advanced alloy that covers the exterior of our ship will withstand any of their attempts to blast their way in. Our hull can withstand collisions with a large asteroid, even a small comet, but we should not allow them to fire those weapons. If any part of the hull is damaged, it will be self-repaired. This ship can place a force field around the whole hull if ordered to do so."

Caden queried, "Should we respond or give some sign of our harnessed power capability?"

Sugrim answered, "We could blind their planetary system by knocking out their satellites—or just prevent them from working." He continued, "If they get close enough to try to get on board, we can cause the ship to send a small signal of a pushback using its force field. Such a slight retaliation should let the earthlings know that we know they are there. It would also reveal that we chose not to contact them. Why not prevent them from coming closer by spreading a force field of, say, fifty kilometres around the ship? The important thing is that we must not let them see us or know who we are."

He continued, "Our physical life forms should not be available to them under any circumstances. To them we will appear as giants, which would cause fear and be intimidating. It is possible that they may panic. Then those nuclear devices may be used in a defensive reaction."

Caden asked, "What are my options should they use their nuclear devices from the circulating drones?"

Sugrim responded, "We could strengthen the force field so it will return the explosive device to its original location. They are unmanned drones, so no human will be hurt. Only a drone or several will be destroyed by their own missiles."

Caden said, "If you are certain of the power that our ship has, then make it happen, but please have a backup plan. The integrity of our ship is vital, and I have no intention of lettings humans do any damage to our home. In the event of a breach, I shall have the ship retaliate with all its protective force, using weapons that I saw during my internship. I have had brief training on their use. That decision will be out of my hands as the safety of our crew takes precedence."

Sugrim answered, "That is a wise decision, Commander. I have programmed the response that you have asked of me. I also feel after their first salvo, we should blind the planet by knocking out their 'eyes' on the cosmos, which euphemistically means their satellites."

Caden said, "Sugrim, since you are in charge of all these measures and understand the powerful self-preservation protocol of our vessel, I would like our crew to see what is happening outside our ship. They need to know what we are up against. And since we have never had to battle any hostiles in our history, they should have an idea as to how we would protect ourselves if the need ever arose."

Sugrim replied, "That is a worthwhile suggestion. I shall use the same technology that we are currently employing for our senior staff and open the view of planet Earth to all members of our crew."

# CHAPTER 33

# Alien Discussions

Commander Caden and his advisory staff returned to their study of the cold files left by Commander Sitla.

The files, while detailed enough, left sections open to speculation and hypothesis. The document read as follows:

> The staff understood under the current siege. They had to monitor the situation on planet Earth. The circumstances have changed since a few of the early citizens of Sig had chosen earlier to remain and settle on this planet. Those who did so found spouses from amongst the primitives and continued working without the technological tools once available to them. The tools were removed when the old ship left and when the newly built duplicate ship left this quadrant of the universe. Most important of all was that the

guidance of our aged professionals was missed. Many had died, and younger replacements had gone with both the old ship and the new one.

Implications: The hybrids, the offspring of these early settlers, must have survived, but over time the original pioneers died. However, our genes have been passed along to following generations.

Sig 3 spoke up: "We have no way of scanning the whole population before we take action. If there are hybrids, it would be unethical to attack our family connections—even though we had nothing to do with the current situation."

Sugrim called for their attention. "Commander Caden, here comes the first nuclear missile." The Commander stood up and watched as the fast-moving point of light followed a laser beam aimed at the hull of the ship. The speed of approach caught the Commander by surprise. Approximately fifty kilometres away, it stopped and was flung backwards, destroying the drone that had fired it.

Almost immediately, hundreds of drones fired together. The explosions that followed were astounding to Caden and his crew. The huge spaceship slightly shivered at the explosions taking place just fifty kilometres away. Needless to say, all Earth drones were destroyed.

# CHAPTER 34

# Protector from the Second Dimension

After this first sortie, the talking heads on Earth became the doomsday-Sayers. Arguments began around the planet of "We should have left well enough alone" the panicking reporters instigated contradictory self-serving suggestions that earthlings appeared to be in a state of chaos. However, Earth's community of different countries gathered again under the leadership of the USA and NASA and began to plan strategy as different options were laid out for discussion.

As night fell over earth, the bright reflection of the spaceship could be seen using backyard telescopes. That was when a series of strange blue laser beams appeared from deep space and struck Earth's orbiting satellites. Earth was completely hushed; no communication was available, and industry could not function. However, the resourceful earthlings quietly set out to find and salvage old cable lines buried under the massive oceans that still functioned and connected the continents.

While this was satisfactory to world leaders, it was not enough to prevent chaos among the populations.

Earth became a planet that was dark in terms of light and international voice communication. All daily industry that depended on communications was incapable of functioning, such as air travel, with planes only being able to land by using visibility and therefore limited to daytime flight. Continental air travel came to a halt, and ship travel was limited because of chaos of the traffic and the risk of natural obstacles such as icebergs in the North Sea.

International space authorities verified the satellites were disabled and did not know how or what exactly had caused it. Later, authorities thought it was a result of the blue laser-like beams that fleetingly flashed from the spaceship. Primitive communication began to take place through underwater cables that were active and the awakening of battery-powered systems. The public, who had become totally reliant on their cellphones, were inconvenienced, but slowly the homes regained electrical power by way of solar energy. A slower pace of daily life began as humans learned to cope.

It was the world governments and industries that depended on rapid communication that were greatly affected.

Within the great ship, Commander Caden saw how the Earth's population became distressed. A rather unusual smile crossed his face. Similarly, there was humour from his coleaders still in the conference room. His voice echoed throughout the whole ship as the crew continued to watch, not understanding that the unmanned vehicles had come both to welcome and greet. Confounded by the lack of any response, the adventurous humans employed force from their drones. The unmanned among these were destroyed.

Commander Caden said, "Let these primitives see the power that I have at hand. Our ship could crush this civilization. We do not have to do anything but sit and watch."

Sugrim asked boldly, "Is that your wish, Commander? Do you wish that I give the order for our ship to attack this planet and annihilate the population?"

To the leaders on Earth, lack of a docile response was one thing, but counterattacking and destroying their drones was not an acceptable response, never mind that the drones attacked first. This was akin to starting a war. The earthlings had bravado in the face of war, but there could be no hero as in the films where a single shuttle pilot such as Will Smith destroyed the attacking aliens and saved Earth.

Earth was ill-equipped to fight outside its solar system, much less win. Here was a show of terrible force from an alien ship that remained on the edge of the solar system. Earthlings' curiosity led them to head out with the simplistic thought of welcoming an alien life form. After months of no response, they decided to attack. Until now the spaceship had remained as an innocent bystander.

One British television announcer and talking head gave his opinion long before the attack, saying, "To my way of thinking, if the alien vessel does not respond, then we should leave it alone. We do not wish to meet aliens who might be unfriendly. I am against sending out contact information and hoping good guys will come to find us and all will be wonderful. We do not know what types of life forms are present in the cosmos, so we should leave well enough alone. If we attract bad guys, then they will be far more technologically advanced than we are.

"We have not yet reached the stage of being able to defend ourselves in the cosmos. We are babies starting out, making an attempt at deep space flight, going farther into this unknown and unfathomable cosmos. If these aliens heard our signals and came to see who we are, trust me, they are overwhelmingly more technologically advanced than we are. We have a lot of water and a great deal of resources, for which an alien society might have expended their own to get here. We will be fair game for a takeover."

After the silencing and inactivity of the satellite systems, this reporter expressed his qualms to his local UK audience. "Their power is great, and so is their technology, so why are we tormenting them? These aliens travelled from across the cosmos and have remained quietly outside our solar system, parked there. Yes, they may have been monitoring us or maybe collecting data. In their minds, we are not worth their advancing to Earth. But oh no! We had to go and poke the bear. What are Earth's options now? I believe that we should make contingency plans, then let the aliens take the initiative. We should wait and see if they will come down to Earth."

He continued, "We should have our government front men meet if the aliens desire such a thing to happen. Alternatively, we should increase our stocks of bacterial spores and allow Earth's population to go underground. Let the microbes do the counterattacking for us. Treat our populations using either antibiotics or vaccines. Once the microbes have done their damage, trust me, the aliens will not come to us wanting to be friendly."

*    *    *

Meanwhile, on board the spaceship, Commander Caden underwent a strange shift in personality. Sugrim saw what was happening as the spot of light hovered above the commander's head.

Caden asked, "Did our ship accomplish that task of closing down the humans' satellites, and did you program that as a one-time task because I asked you?"

Sugrim replied, "Commander, I was brought here to serve the spaceship of Sig under the commander's instructions. Those were my orders from the senate. What is your wish now?"

Caden said, "I would like to see what chaos has been wrought on Earth as a result of your action under my command."

Sugrim answered, "So be it. You will have night vision, Sir."

Immediately Caden and his chosen group saw the human population in the dark, trying to find their way. On the half of the planet with daylight, the governments could not get word out to their citizens as to what had happened. The lights of the cities became dim as televisions across the globe remained dark. While many homes had food and water, the citizens remained listless, almost paralyzed, because they could not get information on what was happening. Slowly solar and wind energy brought some semblance of normal life.

From the shadows of the cities, the worst of the human lower life forms became active and began to break into homes and businesses. There was wide-scale robbing and killing with low-life individuals taking advantage of the darkness. The police and army were unable to do what they'd been trained to do. There were no instructions flowing from the leadership or the governments.

Commander Caden looked on at these activities. He appeared to focus on the damage being done by a few to the many in civilized surroundings. Whatever his feelings were, if he had any, was unknown as he watched, fascinated, with a wry smile on his face. Then, without any warning, his voice echoed, "Well! Shall we let them slowly self-destruct, or shall we remove this vermin infestation from this pristine planet and rid the cosmos of this abomination of our doing?"

It was Sig 2 who answered, saying, "That is a bit unfair, Sir. After all, we caused the chaos you are witnessing below."

Sig 3 said, "It may be that we just brought out the worst in them, but they have the genetic makeup to develop a society where there is inequality among brethren. Such unfairness, since we are the created leaders in the cosmos, should not go unpunished."

Sig 2 replied, "But the punishment should fit the crime. Please remember that it was we who assisted in the creation of these conditions. While we modern citizens of Sig would not have done so, our ancestor was the one who brought about such depravity with one human killing another."

## Penance

"As commander of this vessel," Commander Caden addressed his chosen professionals, "I feel endowed to take power to protect this ship, which is the property of our civilization and our planet, Sig.

"Secondly," he continued, "there is nothing worse than to run away from trouble, which is a form of cowardice. While it is true that the progenitor braves death, he does not do it for any noble reason but to escape from some ill. These humans came and attacked our ship outside their solar system."

Sig 2 said, "Sir! I would like to play the part of devil's advocate here. Will you hear me out, or have you made up your mind?"

Caden replied, "I am still cogitating my options as commander and attempting to carry out what the senate imposed on me, namely, to survive and to keep my crew safe, while continuing our search for a civilized life form close to ours. That was the mission given to me and to every commander who has left Sig over the millennia."

There was a brief silence among this group of officers under the powerful Commander Caden. They all had freedom to speak and to give an opinion based on their qualifications. This latitude was a significant move on the part of the senate on Sig. Its leaders felt that an open session with many minds would provide good support to the commander when he faced difficult decisions. This group would provide him consultation with their qualified minds and honestly trained brains as support.

Sugrim asked, "Commander, have you arrived at a decision?"

Caden answered, "Not as yet, Sugrim, but you should make this management group aware of the powers given to me, which our supertechnological ship will execute at my command."

Sugrim said, "I am sorry, Commander, that is not my mandate."

Caden said, "Sugrim, are you deliberately refusing to do as I order?"

Sugrim replied, "I have a set mandate, which I have explained to you. I am not under your command but under that of the senate of Sig. However, what lies in your power to do lies also in your power not to do."

Caden declared, "What utter nonsense, Sugrim of the holy light; everyone on this ship is under my command. We are no longer under the senate guidance of Sig out here across the cosmos. You will do as I order."

Sugrim responded, "Without prejudice, Sir: the wise leader does not expose himself deliberately to danger since there are few things for which he cares sufficiently. A leader is willing, in great crisis, to give his life, knowing that under certain circumstances it is not worthwhile to live."

Caden said, "Be gone, Sugrim. You are not my conscience. How dare you give such counsel to me? I did not ask it of you. You, like this ship, are a tool under my command, and only I have the power to execute what my desire is. The same is true for all the crew on board."

Sugrim replied, "My apologies, Sir. It was my intention to assist you in making a prudent decision based on the facts at hand. Such facts are always the result of high intention, sincere effort and of course intelligent execution. It is the wise choice among many alternatives. Sir, it is choice, not chance, that makes a determination when a leader has the destiny of many in his hands."

Caden said, "I understand the moral dilemma that you have now placed on me, but I also have a responsibility to correct what one demented commander of our historic past, many light years earlier, tried to redesign the cosmos. That was delusional, and I am here to correct what was done so many light years ago. Give the control of the ship to me now, Sugrim!"

Without any further discussion, Sugrim, replied quietly, "It is under your command, Commander."

"Super ship of Sig, I am Commander Caden, and you are now under my command. I ask that you selectively prepare weapons to terminate all human life forms on planet Earth below. This task must be done without damage to the natural flora and fauna."

Suddenly the ship shivered violently as it kicked into activity; internal lighting came on throughout the ship. The massive spaceship turned to enter the solar system, heading for Earth. As it did so, there was a severe blast that struck the massive ship from behind. The ship turned around rapidly to face the attacker behind its hull. All in the meeting room began to reel at the rapid response of the ship protecting itself. This was the worst they had ever been shaken, and that included the many times when the ship had been struck by large asteroids.

With the still transparent hull, the ship's vision cleared in time for all to see a large opening in the time-space continuum like a blinding flash of lightning against the darkness of space. They saw a huge ship with massive scorched black-stained marks on its tremendous hull, which indicated it was battle-scarred, hurtling towards them.

Caden shouted, "Ship, protect yourself and return full fire at the attacker."

The ship responded and fired volleys with vehemence, but the attacker continued towards them. Just then a booming voice echoed in Caden's ship, "Leave my children alone!" as another great blast rocked Caden's giant technological ship. It shuddered. Caden shouted, "Sugrim, get our ship to respond and protect itself against these earthlings!"

Sugrim's strangled voice replied, "Commander, it is not the earthlings who are attacking; it is a monster from another dimension. It is bearing down on us savagely. Our ship has taken defensive action and is rapidly moving into deep space away from this solar system and into the stream of planets coursing through the cosmos. It is incapable of fighting against this formidable force."

There was another blast, but Caden's ship fired back with almost equal power. Then the sound of an awesome voice penetrated the bowels of Caden's ship:

"Remove yourself from this part of the cosmos, never to return. Leave my children alone. I am Commander Sitla of Sig and of the second dimension. Depart or die!"

# EPILOGUE

In a quiet suburban home, in a cluttered office, an elderly couple sat and sipped hot tea.

Alice commented, "I have lost track of where you were in documenting our understanding of these antique materials. The literature does support your theory in part, you know."

Les her husband replied, "Oh! Do not try to encourage me, Dear. I am a loony. That is why I write science fiction. I can own up to my critical Scots colleague who whispered behind my back, 'What he writes is a load of shit,' to his close friends. They all giggled behind my back after we left the restaurant. Worst of all, I paid the bill for my 'friends.'"

Laughter broke out between the two companions, who had been together for over sixty years. They laughed so hard that their croaky voices broke. After a bit of coughing and blowing of noses, they sat back and sipped their tea.

Les continued as if starting a new discussion: "I have completed my novel. It will be sent to be published after you have a quick gander at the manuscript. Our friend Johnson will have his company assist with the costs of publishing it. Do not worry, our pensions will not be hit too hard; after all, it is our publishing company."

Alice again asked, "Well, are you going to tell me the end? You know, before I begin reading that massive tome of yours!"

Les responded, "Well, yes! The principle behind our months of research is that there are many markers and pointers that lead modern-day archaeologists to suggest that early humankind was in fact responsible. Why such appeasing rubbish? these wonderful structures had a refinement and used a thoughtful science of which primitive humankind was incapable."

Shaking his head, he looked down at the floor absent-mindedly. "The fact is, no work is done to interpret the runes or the languages. They have been left as indecipherable. The university science departments are useless in demanding these tasks be undertaken by the department of ancient languages. It is just passing the buck."

He looked up to see vivid brown eyes staring seriously at him. "You see, Love, it is just another book that will sit on a bookshelf, like so many others that will never be read or, worse, reread. Books are our best friends, for wherever we leave them, they remain unmoved, waiting patiently. Wherever you left off, when you open the pages again, it will be exactly where you left it. Books will never change because their stories and messages remain constant. It is the only true love, between the human reader and the lovely words that inspire imagination.

"Books tell the truth. Those early alien visitors knew that the written word was the way to leave substance and knowledge for the future storytellers, allowing humankind's curiosity to do the rest. They knew intrinsically that we are storytellers; it's in our genes."

Somewhere in deep space, unseen and unheard, an undocumented violent battle ensued between two titans. Earthlings, over time, began to forget the huge ship that sat just outside their solar system many years earlier.

# OTHER WORKS BY DARRYL GOPAUL

## Books

*Bacteria: The Good, the Bad, the Ugly*

*Tales of Myths and Fantasy*

*Around the World on Three Underwear*

*Six Decades to Wisdom … (Maybe)*

*Sonnets of a Human Soul—a Book of Poems*

*A Collection of Fables and Tales*

*Diagnosis*

*Adventures in the Cosmos*

*Imaginary Epics from the Cosmos*

Science fiction trilogy from the novel *Escape from Jipadara:*

*Evolution*
*Tribulations*
*Revelations*

*Glossary of Poems*
*Encyclopedia Library* (e-book only)
*The Biological Key* (e-book only)
*Caravan Boy*
*Mystical Onyx Cubes and an Ancient Manuscript*

## Short Stories

(Created for TV and as small independent movies)

From *Trinidad Tales of Myths and Fantasy*:

"Aunt Lucy Saw the Devil"

"Do Not Mess with the Devil's Handbook"

"Hello! I Am Back (From the Dead, of Course)"

"La Diablesse, Soucouyant and Bois Bandy"

Science fiction, from *Space Academy*:

"Proto"

"Strange Encounter—Parallel Dimension"

And others:

"The Request"

"Oakridge Fen"

"Immunologist"

"Chasing After My Shade"

"The Golden Infidel"

"Soliloquy"

"Luiz's Odyssey"

"There Is a Duck on My Roof"

"Guru Ramesh"

# ABOUT THE BOOK

This is a tale involving human imagination that tries to describe the massive progress of humankind throughout its rapid and unusual evolution. If the dates of the astrophysicists are to be believed, the findings of antiquity do not tangibly reveal the developed skills necessary for the innovative advancements attributed to our primitive past. The words of the anthropologists should be taken with a grain of salt, even while some parts of archaeology may have a grain of speculative truth.

The author in this story is the progenitor of facts that he seems to prefer from his research of literature. He understands the need for a critic or protagonist in his profession of novel writing. No one would better serve this role than his closest companion, that is, his wife of many decades.

There are others in the same position so as not to be totally conceited, not that his relationship is exclusive or special.

What is special is the ability to use daily routines that come along in a lovely quiet retirement of the couple's choosing. "Yes, we have been fortunate to enjoy many benefits after years of hard work, but by far the best benefit is this hobby of storytelling that is found in all our novels."

# ABOUT THE AUTHOR

A retired medical microbiologist and lab scientist with over a hundred peer-reviewed publications and greater than a thousand scholarly addresses delivered globally, Darryl Gopaul began writing short stories secretly over forty years ago. His qualifications include an MBA and a PhD, along with many other degrees. To date, he has written 20 books and enjoys his retirement with his spouse of 53 years in London, Ontario, Canada.

# ABOUT THE BOOK 2

A Tale Clouded in Mystery

"Imagination is more important than knowledge," said Albert Einstein, scientist and mathematician.

When one adds imagination to current observations and success in the exploration of space, one deduces that earthlings will be exploring the cosmos within 50 years. Advanced mathematics, the hard sciences and technological advances continue to leave fewer and fewer things unknown. However, the human psyche is complex. This short series of stories by author Darryl Gopaul appears to explore aspects of the human role in the universe. From Gopaul's powerful imagination, the stories are tightly wound and have much to excite readers of mystery.

This established author is a man who has the gift of storytelling, especially in the genre of science fiction. Readers are kept in an abstract frame of mind as he weaves the tale from unusual perspectives.

Our storyteller exploits visions transmitted across the solar system. He implies there is some all-powerful immortal force that makes the welfare of humankind a priority.

A special author in this genre—Darryl Gopaul.

With Gopaul's intellect, love of storytelling, and knowledge of the hard sciences, he has much to say. Readers are lucky to be exposed to this creator who is just discovering his prowess as a writer, documenter, commentator and practitioner of the human condition.

Darryl Gopaul is a medical microbiologist with a PhD and an MBA. He attacks his tales with vigour.